Nora Ro
of more than on... ...s. A born
storyteller, she creates a blend of warmth, humour and
poignancy that speaks directly to her readers and has
earned her almost every award for excellence in her
field. The youngest of five children, Nora Roberts lives in
western Maryland. She has two sons.

Visit her website at www.noraroberts.com.

Also available by
Nora Roberts

THE MACKADE BROTHERS
The Return of Rafe MacKade
The Pride of Jared MacKade
The Heart of Devin MacKade
The Fall of Shane MacKade

THE STANISLASKIS
Taming Natasha
Falling for Rachel
Luring a Lady
Convincing Alex
Waiting for Nick
Considering Kate

THE CALHOUN WOMEN
The Calhouns:
Catherine, Amanda & Lilah
The Calhouns:
Suzanna & Megan

CORDINA'S ROYAL FAMILY
Affaire Royale
Command Performance
The Playboy Prince
Cordina's Crown Jewel

THE MacGREGORS
Playing the Odds
Tempting Fate
All the Possibilities
One Man's Art
The MacGregors:
Daniel & Ian
The MacGregor Brides:
Christmas Fairytales
The MacGregor Grooms
The Perfect Neighbour
Rebellion

THE STARS OF MITHRA
Stars
Treasures

THE DONOVAN LEGACY
Captivated
Entranced

Charmed
Enchanted

NIGHT TALES
Night Shift
Night Shadow
Nightshade
Night Smoke
Night Shield

THE O'HURLEYS
The Last Honest Woman
Dance to the Piper
Skin Deep
Without a Trace

Time and Again
Reflections
Dance of Dreams
Boundary Lines
Going Home
Dream Makers
Love By Design
Risky Business
The Welcoming
The Right Path
Partners
The Art of Deception
The Winning Hand
Irish Rebel
The Law is a Lady
Table for Two
Summer Pleasures
Under Summer Skies
California Summer
Hazy Summer Nights
Christmas Angels
The Gift
Winter Dreams
The Magic of Home
Catching Snowflakes
Christmas Magic
Night Moves
Dual Image
Summer Dreams

Nora Roberts

Affaire Royale

This edition published in Great Britain 2014
by Mills & Boon, an imprint of Harlequin (UK) Limited,
Eton House, 18-24 Paradise Road, Richmond, Surrey, TW9 1SR

© 1986 Nora Roberts

ISBN: 978-0-263-24643-8

029-0814

Harlequin (UK) Limited's policy is to use papers that are natural, renewable and recyclable products and made from wood grown in sustainable forests. The logging and manufacturing processes conform to the legal environmental regulations of the country of origin.

Printed and bound by
CPI Group (UK) Ltd, Croydon, CR0 4YY

To Marianne Willman
because she understands fairy tales

Prologue

She'd forgotten why she was running. All she knew was that she couldn't stop. If she stopped, she'd lose. It was a race where there were only two places. First and last.

Distance. Every instinct told her to keep running, keep going so that there was distance between her and...where she'd been.

She was wet, for the rain was pounding down, but she no longer jumped at the boom of thunder. Flashes of lightning didn't make her tremble. The dark wasn't what frightened her. She was long past fear of such simple things as the spread of darkness or the violence of the storm. What she feared wasn't clear any longer, only the fear itself. Fear, the only emotion she understood, crawled inside her, settling there as if she'd known nothing else. It was enough to keep her stumbling along the side of the road when her body screamed to lie down in a warm, dry place.

She didn't know where she was. She didn't know where she'd been. There was no memory of the tall, wind-whipped trees. The crash and power of the sea close by meant nothing, nor did the scent of the rain-drenched flowers she crushed underfoot as she fled along the side of a road she didn't know.

She was weeping, but unaware of it. Sobs wracked her, clawing at the fear, doubling it so that it sprinted through her in the absence of everything else. Her mind was so clouded, her legs so unsteady. It would be easy to simply curl up under one of those trees and give up. Something pushed her on. Not just fear, not just confusion. Strength—though one wouldn't guess it to look at her, though she herself didn't recognize it—drove her beyond endurance. She wouldn't go back to where she'd been, so there was no place to go but on.

How long she'd been running wasn't important. She'd no idea whether it'd been one mile or ten. Rain and tears blinded her. The lights were nearly on her before she saw them.

Panicked, like a rabbit caught in the beams, she froze.

They'd found her. They'd come after her. They. The horn blasted, tires squealed. Submitting at last, she crumpled onto the road, unconscious.

Chapter 1

"She's coming out of it."

"Thank God."

"Sir, you must step back for a moment and let me examine her. She may just be drifting again."

Over the mists she was swimming in, she heard the voices. Hollow, distant. Fear scrambled through her. Even in her half-conscious state her breath began to catch. She hadn't escaped. But the fear wouldn't show. She promised herself that. As she came closer to the surface, she closed her hands into tight fists. The feel of her fingers against her palms gave her some sense of self and control.

Slowly she opened her eyes. Her vision ebbed, clouded,

then gradually cleared. So, as she stared into the face bending over her, did the fear.

The face wasn't familiar. It wasn't one of them. She'd know, wouldn't she? Her confidence wavered a moment, but she remained still. This face was round and pleasant, with a trim, curling white beard that contrasted with the smooth, bald head. The eyes were shrewd, tired, but kind. When he took her hand in his, she didn't struggle.

"My dear," he said in a charming, low-key voice. Gently he ran a finger over her knuckles until her fingers relaxed. "You're quite safe."

She felt him take her pulse, but continued to stare into his eyes. Safe. Still cautious, she let her gaze wander away from his. Hospital. Though the room was almost elegant and quite large, she knew she was in a hospital. The room smelled strongly of flowers and antiseptics. Then she saw the man standing just to the side.

His bearing was militarily straight and he was impeccably dressed. His hair was flecked with gray, but it was still very dark and full. His face was lean, aristocratic, handsome. It was stern, she thought, but pale, very pale compared to the shadows under his eyes. Despite his stance and dress, he looked as though he hadn't slept in days.

"Darling." His voice shook as he reached down to take her free hand. There were tears under the words as he pressed her fingers to his lips. She thought she felt the hand, which was strong and firm, tremble lightly. "We have you back now, my love. We have you back."

She didn't pull away. Compassion forbade it. With her hand lying limply in his, she studied his face a second time. "Who are you?"

The man's head jerked up. His damp eyes stared into hers. "Who—"

"You're very weak." Gently the doctor cut him off and drew her attention away. She saw him put a hand on the man's arm, in restraint or comfort, she couldn't tell. "You've been through a great deal. Confusion's natural at first."

Lying flat on her back, she watched the doctor send signals to the other man. A raw sickness began to roll inside her stomach. She was warm and dry, she realized. Warm and dry and empty. She had a body, and it was tired. But inside the body was a void. Her voice was surprisingly strong when she spoke again. Both men responded to it.

"I don't know where I am." Beneath the doctor's hand her pulse jerked once, then settled. "I don't know who I am."

"You've been through a great deal, my dear." The doctor spoke soothingly while his brain raced ahead. Specialists, he thought. If she didn't regain her memory in twenty-four hours, he'd need the best.

"You remember nothing?" The other man had straightened at her words. Now, with his ramrod stance, his sleep-starved eyes direct, he looked down at her.

Confused and fighting back fear, she started to push herself up, and the doctor murmured and settled her back against the pillows. She remembered…running, the storm, the dark. Lights coming up in front of her. Closing her eyes tight, she struggled for composure without knowing why it was so important to retain it. Her voice was still strong, but achingly hollow when she opened them again. "I don't know who I am. Tell me."

"After you've rested a bit more," the doctor began. The other man cut him off with no more than a look. And the look, she saw at a glance, was both arrogant and commanding.

"You're my daughter," he said. Taking her hand again, he held it firmly. Even the light trembling had stopped. "You are Her Serene Highness Gabriella de Cordina."

Nightmare or fairy tale? she wondered as she stared up at him. Her father? Her Serene Highness? Cordina… She thought she recognized the name and clung to it, but what was this talk of royalty? Even as she began to dismiss it, she watched his face. This man wouldn't lie.

His face was passive, but his eyes were so full of emotion she was drawn to them even without memory.

"If I'm a princess," she began, and the dry reserve in her voice caused a flicker of emotion to pass over his face briefly. Amusement? she wondered. "Does that make you a king?"

He nearly smiled. Perhaps the trauma had confused her memory, but she was still his Brie. "Cordina is a principality. I am Prince Armand. You're my eldest child. You have two brothers, Alexander and Bennett."

Father and brothers. Family, roots. Nothing stirred. "And my mother?"

This time she read the expression easily: pain. "She died when you were twenty. Since then you've been my official hostess, taking on her duties along with your own. Brie." His tone softened from the formal and dispassionate. "We call you 'Brie.'" He turned her hand up so that the cluster of sapphires and diamonds on her right hand glimmered toward her. "I gave you this on your twenty-first birthday, nearly four years ago."

She looked at it, and at the strong, beautiful hand that held hers. She remembered nothing. But she felt— trust. When she lifted her eyes again, she managed a half smile. "You have excellent taste, Your Highness."

He smiled, but she thought he was perilously close to

weeping. As close as she. "Please," she began for both their sakes. "I'm very tired."

"Yes, indeed." The doctor patted her hand as he had, though she didn't know it, since the day she'd been born. "For now, rest is the very best medicine."

Reluctantly Prince Armand released his daughter's hand. "I'll be close."

Her strength was already beginning to ebb. "Thank you." She heard the door close, but sensed the doctor hovering. "Am I who he says I am?"

"No one knows better than I." He touched her cheek, more from affection than the need to check her temperature. "I delivered you. Twenty-five years ago in July. Rest now, Your Highness. Just rest."

Prince Armand strode down the corridor in his quick, trained gait, as a member of the Royal Guard followed two paces behind. He wanted to be alone. God, how he wanted five minutes to himself in some closed-off room. There he could let go of some of the tension, some of the emotion that pulled at him. His daughter, his treasure, had nearly been lost to him. Now that he had her back, she looked at him as though he were a stranger.

When he found who—Armand dismissed the thought. It was for later. He promised himself that.

In the spacious, sun-splashed waiting room were three more Royal Guards and several members of Cordina's police department. Pacing, smoking, was his son and heir, Alexander. He had his father's dark, clean-lined looks and military bearing. He did not, as yet, have his father's meticulous control.

Like a volcano, Armand thought, looking at the twenty-three-year-old prince, that simmers and bubbles, but doesn't quite erupt.

Sprawled across a plush, rose-colored sofa was Bennett. At twenty he threatened to become the newest playboy prince. Though he, too, was dark, his looks reflected the heartbreaking beauty of his mother. Though he was often reckless, too often indiscreet, he had an unflagging compassion and kindness that endeared him to his subjects and the press. As well as the female population of Europe, Armand thought wryly.

Beside Bennett was the American who was there at Armand's request. Both princes were too wrapped in their own thoughts to notice their father's presence. The American missed nothing. That's why Armand had sent for him.

Reeve MacGee sat silently for a moment, watching the prince take in the scene. He was holding up well, Reeve thought, but, then, he'd expected no less. He'd only met Cordina's ruler a handful of times, but Reeve's father had been at Oxford with him, where a friendship and mutual respect had been established that had lasted through the years and over the distances.

Armand had gone on to become the ruler of a small, charming country snuggled on the Mediterranean. Reeve's father had become a diplomat. Though he'd grown up with politics and protocol, Reeve had chosen a more behind-the-scenes career for himself. Undercover.

After ten years of dealing with the less elite portion of the nation's capital, Reeve had turned in his badge and started his own private business. There'd come a time in his life when he'd grown tired of following other people's rules. His own were often even more strict, more unbending, but they were his own. The experience he'd gained in Homicide, and then in Special Services had taught him to trust his own instincts first.

He'd been born wealthy. He'd added to his wealth through his own skill. Once he'd looked at his profession as a means of income and a means of excitement. Reeve no longer worked for money. He took few jobs, a select few. If, and only if, something intrigued him, he accepted the client and the responsibility. To the outside world, and often to himself, he was only a farmer, a novice at that. Less than a year before, he'd bought a farm with thoughts, dreams, perhaps, of retiring there. It was, for him, an answer. Ten years of dealing with good and bad, law and disorder on a daily basis had been enough.

Telling himself he'd paid his dues, he'd dropped out of public service. A private detective could pick and choose his clients. He could work at his own pace, name his own fee. If a job led him into danger, he could deal with it in his own fashion. Still, during this past year he'd taken on fewer and fewer of his private cases. He was easing himself out. If he'd had qualms, no one knew of them but himself. The farm was a chance for a different kind of life. One day, he'd promised himself, it would be his whole life. He'd postponed his first shot at spring planting to answer Armand's request.

He looked more like a soldier than a farmer. When he rose at Armand's entrance, his long, rangy body moved subtly, muscle by muscle. The neat linen jacket was worn over a plain T-shirt and trim slacks, but he could give them the air of formality or casualness as he chose. He was the kind of man whose clothes, no matter how attractive, were noticed only after he was. His face drew the attention first, perhaps because of the smooth good looks he'd inherited from his Scotch-Irish ancestors. His skin would have been pale if he hadn't spent so much time out of doors. His dark hair was cut well, but insisted on falling over his brow. His mouth was wide and tended to look serious.

His bone structure was excellent and his eyes were the charming, sizzling blue of the Black Irish. He'd used them to charm when it suited him, just as he'd used them to intimidate.

His stance was less rigid than the prince's, but no less watchful. "Your Highness."

At Reeve's words, both Alexander and Bennett sprang to attention. "Brie?" they asked together, but while Bennett was already beside his father, Alexander stood where he was. He crushed out his cigarette in an ashtray. Reeve watched it snap in two.

"She was conscious," Armand said briefly. "I was able to speak with her."

"How does she feel?" Bennett looked at his father with dark, concerned eyes. "When can we see her?"

"She's very tired," Armand said, touching his son's arm only lightly. "Perhaps tomorrow."

Still at the window, Alexander smoldered. "Does she know who— "

"That's for later," his father cut him off.

Alexander might have said more, but his upbringing had been too formal. He knew the rules and the restrictions that went with his title. "We'll take her home soon," he said quietly, coming very close to challenging his father. He cast a quick look around at the guards and police. Gabriella might be protected here, but he wanted her home.

"As soon as possible."

"She may be tired," Bennett began, "but she'll want to see a familiar face later on. Alex and I can wait."

A familiar face. Armand looked beyond his son to the window. There were no familiar faces for his Brie. He'd explain to them, but later, in private. For now, he could only be the prince. "You may go." His words took in both his sons. "Tomorrow she'll be more rested. Now I need a word with Reeve." He dismissed his sons without a gesture. When they hesitated, he lifted a brow. It was not, as it could have been, done with heat.

"Is she in pain?" Alexander blurted out.

Armand's look softened. Only someone who knew him well would have seen it. "No. I promise you. Soon," he added when Alexander remained unsatisfied, "you'll see for yourself. Gabriella is strong." It was said with a simplicity that was filled with pride.

With a nod, Alexander accepted. What else he had to say would have to wait for a private moment. He walked out with his brother, flanked by guards.

Armand watched his sons, then turned to Reeve. "Please," he began, and gestured. "We'll use Dr. Franco's office for a moment." He moved across the corridor and down as though he didn't notice the guards. Reeve did. He felt them close and tense. A royal kidnapping, he mused, tended to make people nervous. Armand opened a door, waited until Reeve was inside, then closed it again.

"Sit, please," he invited. "I can't just yet." Reaching into his pocket, he drew out a dark-brown cigarette, one of the ten he permitted himself daily. Before he could do so himself, Reeve lit it and waited. "I'm grateful you came, Reeve. I haven't had the opportunity to tell you how I appreciate it."

"There's no need to thank me, Your Highness. I haven't done anything yet."

Armand blew out smoke. He could relax, just a little, in front of the son of his friend. "You think I'm too hard on my sons."

"I think you know your sons better than I."

Armand gave a half laugh and sat. "You have your father's diplomatic tongue."

"Sometimes."

"You have, also, if I see clearly, his clear and clever mind."

Reeve wondered if his father would appreciate the comparison, and smiled. "Thank you, Your Highness."

"Please, in private, it must be Armand." For the first time since his daughter had awoken, his emotions slipped. With one hand he kneaded the skin just above his eyebrows. The band of tension there could be ignored for only so long. "I think I'm about to impose on your father's friendship through you, Reeve. I think, because of my love for my daughter, I have no other choice."

Reeve measured the man who sat across from him. Now he saw more than the royalty. He saw a father desperately hanging on to control. In silence, Reeve took out a cigarette of his own, lit it and gave Armand just a few more minutes. "Tell me."

"She remembers nothing."

"She doesn't remember who kidnapped her?" With a faint scowl Reeve studied the toe of his shoe. "Did she see them at all?"

"She remembers nothing," Armand repeated, and lifted his head. "Not even her own name."

Reeve took in all the implications, and their consequences. He merely nodded, showing none of the thoughts that formed and raced through his mind. "Temporary amnesia would be common enough after what she's been through, I imagine. What does the doctor say?"

"I will speak to him shortly." The strain, having gone on for six days, wore on him, but he didn't allow it to come through in his voice. "You came, Reeve, because I asked you. Yet you never asked me why."

"No."

"As an American citizen, you're under no obligation to me."

Reeve blew out a thin stream of Virginia tobacco to mix with the French of Armand's. "No."

Armand's lips curved. Like his father, the prince thought. And like his father, Reeve MacGee could be trusted. He was about to trust him with his most prized possession. "In my position, there is always a certain element of danger. You understand this."

"Any leader lives with it."

"Yes. And, by birth and proximity, a leader's children." For a moment he looked down at his hands, at the ornate gold ring of his office. He was, by birth, a prince. He was also a father. Still, he'd never had a choice about which came first. He'd been born, educated and molded to rule. Armand had always known his first obligation was to his people.

"Naturally, my children have their own personal security." With a kind of controlled violence, he crushed out his cigarette. "It seems that it is inadequate. Brie— Gabriella—is often impatient with the need for guards. She's stubborn about her privacy. Perhaps I've spoiled her. We're a peaceful country, Reeve. The Royal Family of Cordina is loved by its citizens. If my daughter slipped away from her guards from time to time, I made little of it."

"Is that what happened this time?"

"She wanted to drive in the country. It's something

she does from time to time. The responsibilities of her title are many. Gabriella needs an escape valve. Until six days ago, it seemed like a very harmless one, which was why I permitted it."

The very tone told Reeve that Armand ruled his family as he did his country, with a just, but cool hand. He absorbed the feeling as easily as he did the information. "Until six days ago," Reeve repeated. "When your daughter was abducted."

Armand nodded calmly. There were facts to be dealt with; emotion only clouded them. "Now, until we're certain who abducted her and why, she can't be allowed something so harmless. I would trust the Royal Guards with my life. I can't trust them with my daughter's."

Reeve tapped out his cigarette gently. The drift was coming across loud and clear. "I'm not on the force any longer, Armand. And you don't want a cop."

"You have your own business. I understand you're something of an expert on terrorism."

"In my own country," Reeve pointed out. "I certainly have no credentials in Cordina." He felt his curiosity pick up another notch. Impatient with himself, he frowned at Armand. "I've had the opportunity to make contacts over the years. I could give you the names of some good men. If you're looking for a royal bodyguard—"

"I'm looking for a man I can trust with my daughter's life," Armand interrupted. He said it quietly, but the thread of power lay just beneath. "A man I can trust to remain as objective as I myself must remain. A man who has had experience dealing with a potentially explosive situation with…finesse. I've followed your career." He gave another quick smile at Reeve's bland look. "I have a few connections in Washington. Your record was exemplary, Reeve. Your father can be proud of you."

Reeve shifted uncomfortably at the mention of his father. The connection was too damn personal, he thought. It would make it more difficult for him to accept and be objective, or to refuse graciously—guiltlessly. "I appreciate that. But I'm not a cop. I'm not a bodyguard. I'm a farmer."

Armand's expression remained grave, but Reeve caught the quick light of humor in his eyes. "Yes, so I've been told. If you prefer, we can leave it at that. However, I have a need. A great need. I won't press you now." Armand knew when to advance and when to retreat. "Give some thought to what I've said. Tomorrow, perhaps we can talk again, and you can speak with Gabriella yourself. In the meantime, you are our guest." He rose, signaling an end to the interview. "My car will take you back to the palace. I will remain here a bit longer."

The late-morning sunlight filtered into the room. Vaguely wanting a cigarette, Reeve watched its patterns on the floor. He'd spoken with Armand again, over a private breakfast in the prince's suite. If there was one thing Reeve understood, it was quiet determination and cold power. He'd grown up with it.

Swearing lightly, Reeve looked through the window at the mountains that cupped Cordina so beautifully.

Why the hell was he here? His land was thousands of miles away and waiting for his plow. Instead he was in this little fairy-tale country where the air was seductively soft and the sea was blue and close. He should never have come, Reeve told himself ruthlessly. When Armand had contacted him, he should simply have made his excuses. When his father had called to add weight to the prince's request, Reeve should have told him he had fields to till and hay to plant.

He hadn't. With a sigh, Reeve admitted why. His father had asked so little of him and had given so much. The friendship that bound Ambassador Francis MacGee to His Royal Highness Armand of Cordina was strong and real. Armand had flown to the States for his mother's funeral. It wasn't possible to forget how much that support had meant to his father.

And he hadn't forgotten the princess. He continued to stare out of the window. The woman slept behind him in the hospital bed, pale, vulnerable, fragile. Reeve remembered her ten years before, when he'd joined his parents for a trip to Cordina.

It had been her sixteenth birthday, Reeve remembered. He'd been in his twenties, already working his way up on the force. He hadn't been a man with illusions. Certainly not one to believe in fairy tales. But that had been exactly what Her Serene Highness Gabriella had been.

Her dress—he could still remember it—had been a pale, mint-colored silk nipped into an impossibly small waist, billowing out like clouds. Against it, her skin had been glowing with life and youth. She'd worn a little ring of diamonds in her hair, glittering, winking, sizzling, against that deep, rich chestnut. It was hair a man wanted to run his fingers through, possessively. Her face had been all roses and cream and delicacy, with a mouth that was full and promising. And her eyes… Reeve remembered them most of all. Her eyes, under dark, arched brows, surrounded by lush, lush lashes, had been like topaz.

Almost reluctantly, he turned to look at her now.

Her face was still delicate, perhaps more so since she'd grown from girl to woman. The sweep of her cheekbones gave her dignity. Her skin was pale, as though the life and youth had been washed out of it. Her hair was still rich, but it was brushed straight back, leaving her face

vulnerable. The beauty was still there, but it was so fragile a man would be afraid to touch.

One arm was thrown across her body, and he could
see the sparkle of diamonds and sapphire. Yet her nails
were short and uneven, as though they'd been bitten or
broken off. The IV still fed into her wrist. He remembered when she was sixteen she'd worn a bracelet of
pearls there.

It was that memory that caused the anger to roll
through him. It had been a week since her abduction,
two days since the young couple had found her collapsed on the side of the road, yet no one knew what
she'd been through. He could remember the scent of her
perfume from ten years before. She couldn't remember
her own name.

Some puzzles could be left on the shelf and easily ignored; some could be speculated on and left to others.
Then there were those that intrigued and tempted. They
called to the part of him that was seduced by questions,
riddles and the often violent way of solving them that,
he'd nearly convinced himself, had been overcome.

Armand had been clever, Reeve thought grimly, very
clever, to insist that he see Princess Gabriella for himself. What was he going to do about her? he asked himself. What in hell was he going to do? He had his own
life to start, the new one he'd chosen for himself. A man

trying for a second beginning didn't have time to mix himself up in other people's problems. Hadn't that been just what he'd wanted to get away from?

His brow was furrowed in the midst of his contemplations; that was how she saw him when she opened her eyes. Brie stared into the grim, furious face, saw the smoldering blue irises, the tight mouth, and froze. What was dream and what was real? she asked herself as she braced herself. The hospital. She allowed her gaze to leave his only long enough to assure herself she was still there. Her fingers tightened on the sheets until they were white, but her voice came calmly.

"Who are you?"

Whatever else had changed about her over the years or over the past week, the eyes were the same. Tawny, deep. Fascinating. Reeve kept his hands in his pockets. "I'm Reeve MacGee, a friend of your father's."

Brie relaxed a little. She remembered the man with the tired eyes and military stance who'd told her he was her father. No one knew how restless and frustrated a night she'd spent trying to find some glimmer of memory. "Do you know me?"

"We met several years ago, Your Highness." The eyes that had fascinated him in the girl, and now in the woman, seemed to devour him. She needs something, he thought. She's groping for any handhold. "It was your sixteenth birthday. You were exquisite."

"You're American, Reeve MacGee?"

He hesitated a moment, his eyes narrowing. "Yes. How do you know?"

"Your voice." Confusion came and went in her eyes. He could almost see her grab on to that one thin thread. "I hear it in your voice. I've been there... Have I been there?"

"Yes, Your Highness."

He knew, she thought. He knew, but she could only guess. "Nothing." Tears welled up and were vanquished. She was too much her father's daughter. "Can you imagine," she began very steadily, "what it is to wake up with nothing? My life is blank pages. I have to wait for others to fill it for me. What happened to me?"

"Your Highness—"

"Must you call me that?" she demanded.

The flash of impatient spirit took him back a pace. He tried not to smile. He tried not to admire it. "No," he said simply, and made himself comfortable on the edge of her bed. "What would you like to be called?"

"By my name." Brie looked down in annoyance at the bandage on her wrist. That would be done away with soon, she decided, then managed to shift herself up. "I'm told it's Gabriella."

"You're more often known as Brie."

She was silent a moment as she struggled to find the familiarity. The blank pages remained blank. "Very well, then. Now tell me what happened to me."

"We don't have the details."

"You must," she corrected, watching him. "If not all, you have some. I want them."

He studied her. Fragile, yes, but under the fragility was a core of strength. She'd have to build on it again. "Last Sunday afternoon you went out for a drive in the country. The next day, your car was found abandoned. There were calls. Ransom calls. Allegedly you'd been abducted and were being held." He didn't add what the threats had been or what would have been done to her if the ransom demands weren't met. Nor did he add that the ransom demands had ranged from exorbitant amounts of money to the release of certain prisoners.

"Kidnapped." Brie's fingers reached out and gripped his. She saw images, shadows. A small, dark room. The smell of...kerosene and must. She remembered the nausea, the headaches. The terror came back, but little else. "It won't come clear," she murmured. "Somehow I know it's true, but there's a film I can't brush away."

"I'm no doctor." Reeve spoke in brisk tones because her fight to find herself affected him too strongly. "But

I'd say not to push it. You'll remember when you're ready
to remember."

"Easy to say." She released his hand. "Someone's stolen my life from me, Mr. MacGee… What's your place
in this?" she demanded suddenly. "Were we lovers?"

His brow lifted. She certainly didn't beat around the
bush, he mused. Nor, he thought, only half-amused, did
she sound too thrilled by the prospect. "No. As I said,
you were sixteen the one and only time we met. Our fathers are old friends. They'd have been a bit annoyed if
I'd seduced you."

"I see. Then why are you here?"

"Your father asked me to come. He's concerned about
your security."

She glanced down at the ring on her finger. Exquisite, she thought. Then she saw her nails and frowned.
That was wrong, wasn't it? she wondered. Why would
she wear such a ring and not take care of her hands?
Another flicker of memory taunted her. Brie closed her
hands into fists as it hovered, then faded. "If my father
is concerned about my security," she continued, unaware
that Reeve watched her every expression, "what is that
to you?"

"I've had some experience with security. Prince Armand has asked me to look out for you."

She frowned again, in a quiet, thoughtful way she

had no idea was habit. "A bodyguard?" She said it in the same impatient way he had. "I don't think I'd like that."

The simple dismissal had him doing a complete reversal. He'd given up his free time, come thousands of miles, and she didn't think she'd like it. "You'll find, Your Highness, that even a princess has to do things she doesn't like. Might as well get used to it."

She studied him blandly, the way she did when her temper threatened her good sense. "I think not, Mr. Mac-Gee. I find myself certain that I wouldn't tolerate having someone hover around me. When I get home—" She stopped, because home was another blank. "When I get home," she repeated, "I'll find another way of dealing with it. You may tell my father that I declined your kind offer."

"The offer isn't to you, but to your father." Reeve rose. This time Brie was able to see that for sheer size he was impressive. His leanness didn't matter, nor did his casually expensive clothes. If he meant to block your way, you'd be blocked. Of that much she was sure.

He made her uneasy. She didn't know why, or, annoyingly, if she should know. Yet he did, and because of this she wanted nothing to do with him on a day-to-day basis. Her life was jumbled enough at the moment without a man like Reeve MacGee in her way.

She asked if they'd been lovers because the idea both

stirred and frightened. When he'd said no, she hadn't felt relief but the same blank flatness she'd been dealing with for two days. Perhaps she was a woman of little emotion, Brie considered. Perhaps life was simpler that way.

"I've been told I'm nearly twenty-five, Mr. MacGee."

"Must you call me that?" he countered, deliberately using the same tone she had. He saw her smile quickly. The light came on and switched off.

"I am an adult," she went on. "I make my own decisions about my life."

"Since you're a member of the Royal Family of Cordina, some of those decisions aren't just yours to make." He walked to the door and, opening it, stood with his hand on the knob. "I've got better things to do, Gabriella, than princess-sit." His smile came quickly, also, and was wry. "But even commoners don't always have a choice."

She waited until the door was closed again, then sat up. Dizziness swept over her. For a moment, just a moment, she wanted to lie back until someone came to help, to tend. But she wouldn't tolerate being tied down any longer. Swinging out of bed, she waited for the weakness to fade. It was something she had to accept for now. Then carefully, slowly, she walked toward the mirror on the far wall.

She'd avoided this. Remembering nothing of her looks, a thousand possibilities had formed in her mind.

Who was she? How could she begin to know when she didn't know the color of her eyes. Taking a steadying breath, she stood in front of the mirror and looked.

Too thin, she thought quickly. Too pale. But not, she added with foolish relief, hideous. Perhaps her eyes were an odd color, but they weren't crossed or beady. Lifting a hand to her face, she traced it. Thin, she thought again. Delicate, frightened. There was nothing in the reflection that resembled the man who was her father. She'd seen strength in his face. In her own she saw frailty— too much of it.

Who are you? Brie demanded as she pressed her palm against the glass. What are you?

Then, despising herself, she gave in to her despair and wept.

Chapter 2

It wasn't something she'd do again, Brie told herself as she stepped out of a hot, soothing shower. She wouldn't bury her face in her hands and cry because things were piling up on her. What she would do, what she would begin to do right now, was to shift them, one at a time. If there were answers to be found, that was the way to find them.

First things first. Brie slipped into the robe she'd found hanging in the closet. It was thick and plush and emerald green. It was also frayed a bit around the cuffs. An old favorite, she decided, accepting the comfort she felt with the robe around her. But the closet had offered her nothing else. Decisively Brie pushed the button and waited for the nurse.

"I want my clothes," Brie said immediately.

"Your Highness, you shouldn't be——"

"I'll speak to the doctor if necessary. I need a hair-brush, cosmetics and suitable clothes." She folded her hands in a gesture that looked commanding, but had more to do with nerves. "I'm going home this morning."

One didn't argue with royalty. The nurse curtsied her way out of the room and went directly for the doctor.

"Now what's all this?" He came bustling into the room, all warmth, all good cheer and patience. She thought of a short, stout brick wall cleverly concealed behind ivy and moss. "Your Highness, you have no business getting up."

"Dr. Franco." It was time, Brie decided, to test herself. "I appreciate your skill and your kindness. I'm going home today."

"Home." His eyes sharpened as he stepped forward. "My dear Gabriella."

"No." She shook her head, denying his unspoken question. "I don't remember."

Franco nodded. "I've spoken to Dr. Kijinsky, Your Highness. He's much more knowledgeable about this condition than I. This afternoon——"

"I'll see your Kijinsky, Dr. Franco, but not this afternoon." She dipped her hands into the deep pockets of the robe and touched something small and slim. Bringing it out, Brie found herself holding a hairpin. She closed her hand tightly over it, as if it might bring something rushing back. "I need to try to figure this out my way. Perhaps if I'm back where things are familiar to me, I'll remember. You assured me yesterday after my...father left, that this memory loss is temporary and that other than fatigue and shock, I have no major injuries. If that's the case, I can rest and recuperate just as well at home."

"Your rest and recuperation can be monitored more efficiently here."

She gave him a quiet, very stubborn smile. "I don't choose to be monitored, Dr. Franco. I choose to go home."

"Perhaps neither of you remembers Gabriella said the same thing only hours after her tonsils were removed." Armand stood in the doorway, watching his delicately built daughter face down the tanklike Franco. Coming in, he held out his hand. Though her hesitation to accept it hurt, he curled his fingers gently over hers. "Her Highness will come home," he said without looking at the doctor. Before Brie could smile, he went on, "You'll give me a list of instructions for her care. If she doesn't follow them, she'll be sent back."

The urge to protest came and went. Something inherent quelled it. Instead she inclined her head. What should have been a subservient movement was offset by the arrogant lift of brow. Armand's fingers tightened on hers as he saw the familiar gesture. She'd given him that look countless times when she'd bargained for and received what she wanted.

"I'll send for your things."

"Thank you."

But she didn't add "father." Both of them knew it.

Within an hour, she was walking out. She liked the cheerful, spring dress splashed with pastels that she was wearing. She had felt both relief and satisfaction when she'd discovered she had a clever hand with cosmetics.

As Brie stepped into the sunlight there was a faint blush of color in her cheeks, and the shadows under her eyes had been blotted out. Her hair was loose, swinging down to brush her shoulders. The scent she'd dabbed on had been unapologetically French and teasing. She found, like the robe, that she was comfortable in it.

She recognized the car as a limo and knew the interior would be roomy and smell rich. She couldn't remember riding in it before, or the face of the driver who smiled and bowed as he ushered her inside. She sat in silence a moment as her father settled in the seat across from her.

"You look stronger, Brie."

There was so much to say, yet she had so little. Details eluded her. Instead there were feelings. She didn't feel odd in the plush quiet of the limo. The weight of the glittery ring she wore was comfortable on her hand. She knew her shoes were Italian, but only the scuffs on the soles showed her that they'd been worn before. By her, certainly. The fit was perfect.

The scent her father wore soothed her nerves. She looked at him again, searching. "I know I speak French as easily as English, because some of my thoughts come in that language," she began. "I know what roses smell like. I know which direction I should look to see the sun rise over the water and what it looks like at dawn. I don't know if I'm a kind person or a selfish one. I don't know the color of the walls of my own room. I don't know if I've done well with my life or if I've wasted it."

It tore at him to watch her sitting calmly across from him, trying to explain why she couldn't give him the love he was entitled to. "I could give you the answers."

She nodded, as controlled as he. "But you won't."

"I think if you find them yourself, you'll find more."

"Perhaps." Looking down, she smoothed her fingers over the white snakeskin bag she carried. "I've already discovered I'm impatient."

Quick, dashing, he grinned. Brie found herself drawn to him, smiling back. "Then you've begun."

"And I have to be satisfied with a beginning."

"My dear Gabriella, I have no illusions that you'll be satisfied with that for long."

Brie glanced at the window as they climbed up, steadily up, a long, winding road. There were many trees, with palms among them, their fronds fluttering. There was rock, gray, craggy rock thrusting out, but wildflowers shoved their way through the cracks. The sea was below, deep, paintbrush blue and serene.

If she looked up, following the direction of the road, she could see the town with its pink and white buildings stacked like pretty toys on the jutting, uneven promontory.

A fairy tale, she thought again, yet it didn't surprise her. As they approached, Brie felt again a sense of quiet comfort. The town lost nothing of its charm on closer contact. The houses and buildings seemed content to push their way out of the side of rock, balanced with one another and the lay of the land. There was an overall tidiness and a sense of age.

No skyscrapers, no frantic rush. Something inside her recognized this, but, she thought, she'd been to cities where the pace was fast and the buildings soared up and up. Yet this was home. She felt no urge to argue. This was home.

"You won't tell me about myself." She looked at Armand again and her eyes were direct, her voice strong. "Tell me about Cordina."

She'd pleased him. Brie could see it in the way his lips

curved just slightly. "We are old," he said, and she heard the pride. "The Bissets—that's our family name—have lived and ruled here since the seventeenth century. Before, Cordina was under many governments, Spanish, Moorish, Spanish again, then French. We are a port, you see, and our position on the Mediterranean is valuable.

"In 1657, another Armand Bisset was granted the principality of Cordina. It has remained in Bisset hands, and will remain so as long as there is a male heir. The title cannot pass to a daughter."

"I see." After a moment's thought Brie tilted her head. "Personally I can be grateful for that, but as a policy, it's archaic."

"So you've said before," he murmured.

"I see." And she saw children playing in a green leafy park where a fountain gushed. She saw a store with glittery dresses in the front, and a bakery window filled with pink and white confections. There was a house where the lawn flamed with azaleas. "And have the Bissets ruled well?"

It was like her to ask, he thought. While she didn't remember, the questing mind remained, and the compassion. "Cordina is at peace," he said simply. "We are a member of the United Nations. I govern, assisted by Loubet, Minister of State. There is the Council of the Crown, which meets three times a year. On international treaties, I must consult them. All laws must be approved by the National Council, which is elected."

"Are there women in the government?"

He lifted a finger to lightly rub his chin. "You haven't lost your taste for politics. There are women," he told her. "Though you wouldn't be satisfied by the percentages, Cordina is a progressive country."

"Perhaps 'progressive' is a relative term."

"Perhaps." He smiled, because this particular debate was an old one. "Shipping is, naturally, our biggest industry, but tourism is not far behind. We have beauty, culture and an enviable climate. We are just," he said with simplicity. "Our country is small, but it is not insignificant. We rule well."

This she accepted without any questions, but if she'd had them, they would have flown from her mind by the sight of the palace.

It stood, as was fitting, on the highest point of Cordina's rocky jut of land. It faced the sea, with huge rocks and sheer cliffs tumbling down to the water.

It was a place King Arthur might have visited, and would recognize if his time came again. The recognition came to Brie the same way everything else had, a vague feeling, as if she were seeing something in a dream.

It was made of white stone and the structure spread out in a jumble of battlements, parapets and towers.

It had been built for both royalty and defense, and remained unchanged. It hovered over the capital like a protection and a blessing.

There were guards at the gate, but the gates weren't closed. In their tidy red uniforms they looked efficient, yet fanciful. Brie thought of Reeve MacGee.

"Your friend spoke to me—Mr. MacGee." Brie tore her gaze away from the palace. Business first, she reflected. It seemed to be her way. "He tells me you've asked for his assistance. While I appreciate your concern, I find the idea of yet another stranger in my life uncomfortable."

"Reeve is the son of my oldest and closest friend. He isn't a stranger." Nor am I, he thought, and willed himself to be patient.

"To me he is. By his own account he tells me we've met only once, almost ten years ago. Even if I could remember him, he'd be a stranger."

He'd always admired the way she could use such clean logic when it suited her. And willfulness when it didn't. Admiration, however, didn't overshadow necessity. "He was a member of the police force in America and handled the sort of security we require now."

She thought of the neat red uniforms at the gate, and the men who sat in the car following the limo. "Aren't there enough guards?"

Armand waited until the driver stopped in front of the entrance. "If there were, none of this would be necessary." He stepped from the car first and turned to assist his daughter himself. "Welcome home, Gabriella."

Her hand remained in his and the light breeze ruffled between them. She wasn't ready to go in. Armand felt it, and waited.

She could smell the flowers now. Jasmine, vanilla, spice, and the roses that grew in the courtyard. The grass was so green, the stone so white it was almost blinding. There had to have been a drawbridge once, she was sure of it. Now there was an arched mahogany door at the top of curved stone steps. Glass, sometimes clear, sometimes tinted, glistened as it should in palaces. At the topmost tower a flag whipped in the wind. Snowy white with an arrogant diagonal slash of red.

Slowly she looked over the building. It tugged at her, welcoming her. The sense of peace wasn't something she imagined. It was as real as the fear she'd felt not long before. Yet she couldn't say which of those sparkling windows were hers. She'd come to find out, Brie reminded herself, and stepped forward.

Even as she did, the wide door was flung open. A young man with dark, thick hair and a dancer's build dashed out. "Brie!" Then he was on her, embracing her with all the strength and enthusiasm of youth. He smelled comfortably of horses. "I'd just come in from the stables when Alex told me you were on your way."

Brie felt the waves of love coming from him, and looked helplessly over his shoulder to her father.

"Your sister needs rest, Bennett."

"Of course. She'll rest better here." Grinning, he drew back, keeping her hands tight in his. He looked so young, she thought, so beautiful, so happy. When he saw her face, his eyes sobered quickly. "You don't remember? Still?"

She wanted to reach out to him. He seemed to need it so. All she could do was return the squeeze of hand to hand. "I'm sorry."

He opened his mouth, then shut it again, slipping an arm around her waist. "Nonsense." His voice was cheerful, but he kept her carefully between himself and their father. "You'll remember soon enough now that you're home. Alex and I thought we'd have to wait until this afternoon to see you in the hospital. This is so much better."

As he spoke he was easing her gently in the front door, talking quickly, she was sure, to put both her and himself at ease. She saw the hall, wide and stunning with its frescoed ceiling and polished floor, the gracious sweep of stairs leading up and up, to what she didn't yet know. Because her heart was pounding, she concentrated on the scents that soothed her. Fresh flowers and lemon wax. She heard the sound of her heels striking the wood and echoing.

There was a tall, glossy urn on a stand. She knew it was Ming, just as she knew the stand was Louis XIV. Things, Brie thought. She could identify them, catalog them, but she couldn't relate herself to them. Sunlight poured through two high arched windows but didn't warm her skin.

Escape. The need for it rolled around inside her. She wanted to turn around and walk out, go back to the safe, impersonal hospital room. There weren't so many demands there, so many of these unspoken questions that hung on the air. She wouldn't feel such an outpouring of love, or the need from those around for her to return it. Had she ever? she wondered. When she remembered who she was, would she find a cold, unfeeling woman?

Bennett felt her tense, and tightened his arm around her. "Everything's going to be all right now, Brie."

From somewhere she found the strength to smile. "Yes, of course."

Several paces down the hall a door opened. Brie knew the man to be her brother only because of the strong resemblance between him and the man at her side. She tried to empty herself so that any emotions she might feel would have room.

He wasn't as smoothly handsome as Bennett. His good looks were more intense and less comfortable than his younger brother's. Though he was young, she sensed the same immovable dignity in him as she did in their father. But of course, she reminded herself. He was the heir. Such things were both a gift and a burden.

"Gabriella." Alex didn't rush to her as Bennett did, but came forward steadily, watching her. When he stood in front of her, he lifted his hands and framed her face. The gesture seemed natural, as if he'd done so time and again in the past. The past, she thought as his fingers were warm and firm on her skin, she didn't have. "We've missed you. No one's shouted at me in a week."

"I…" Floundering, she said nothing. What should she say? What should she feel? She knew only that this was too much and she hadn't been as prepared as she'd thought. Then, over Alexander's shoulder, she saw Reeve.

Obviously he'd been closeted with her brother but had stood back to watch the reunion. Another time she might resent it, but now she found she needed his calm impartiality. Hanging on to control, she touched her brother's hand. "I'm sorry, I'm very tired."

She saw something flicker in Alexander's eyes, but then he stepped back. "Of course you are. You should rest. I'll take you up."

"No." Brie struggled not to let the refusal sound as blunt as it was. "Forgive me, I need some time. Perhaps Mr. MacGee wouldn't mind taking me to my room."

"Brie—"

Bennett's protest was immediately quelled by Armand. "Reeve, you know Gabriella's rooms."

"Of course." He stepped forward and took her arm, but the touch was impersonal. He thought he felt her sigh in relief. "Your Highness?"

He led her away, up the curving stairs, where she paused once to look back down on the three men who watched. She seemed so distant from them, so separated. The pull and tug of emotion came and went, so that she climbed the rest of the stairs in silence.

She recognized nothing in the wide, gleaming corridors, nothing in the exquisite wall hangings or draping curtains. Once they passed a servant whose eyes filled as she stopped and curtsied.

"How is it I'm loved like this?" Brie murmured.

Reeve walked on, his hand barely touching her arm as he guided her. "People generally want to be loved."

"Don't people generally wonder if they deserve it?" With an impatient shake of her head, she went on. "It's as if I've stepped into a body. The body has a past, but I don't. Inside this woman, I look out and see other's reactions to her."

"You could use it to your advantage."

She sent him a quick, interested look. "In what way?"

"You have the advantage of seeing the people around you without having your own emotions color what you see. Observation without prejudice. It might be an interesting way to understand yourself."

She didn't relax so much as accept. "You see now why I asked you to bring me up."

He stopped in front of a beautifully carved door. "Do I?"

"I thought only moments ago that I wanted no more strangers in my life. And yet… You haven't any strong feelings for me and you don't expect them in return. It's easy for you to look at me and be practical."

He studied her now in the misty light of the corridor. It wasn't possible for a man to look at her and think practical thoughts, but it wasn't the time to mention that. "You were frightened downstairs."

She tilted her chin and met his eyes. "Yes."

"So you've decided to trust me."

"No." She smiled then, beautifully. Something of the girl he'd met with diamonds in her hair came through. Too much of the attraction he'd felt crept along with it. "Trust isn't something I can give so quickly under the circumstances."

Perhaps more than the smile, the strength attracted him. "What have you decided, then?"

Perhaps more than his looks, his confidence attracted her. "I don't want your services as a policeman, Reeve, but I think your services as a stranger might be invaluable. My father is determined to have you in any case, so perhaps we might come to an agreement between us."

"Of what kind?"

"I don't want to be hovered over. I think I can be certain that's the one thing that was always true. I'd like to consider you as more of a buffer between me and…"

"Your family?" he finished.

Her lashes swept down and her fingers tightened on her bag. "Don't make it sound so cold."

Touching her would be a mistake. He had to remind himself of that. "You've a right to the time and distance you need, Gabriella."

"They have needs, as well. I'm not unaware of that." Her head came up again, but she looked beyond him to the door. "This is my room?"

For a moment she'd looked so lost, so totally lost. He wanted to offer comfort, but knew it was the last thing she wanted or needed. "Yes."

"Would you think I was a coward if I said I didn't want to go in alone?"

For an answer, he opened the door and walked in just ahead of her.

So, she preferred pastels. As Brie looked around the small, charming sitting room she saw the pale, sun-washed colors. No frills, she noted, rather pleased. Even without them, the room was essentially feminine. She felt a sense of relief that she accepted her womanhood without needing elaborate trappings to prove it. Maybe, just maybe, she'd find she liked Gabriella.

The room wasn't cluttered, nor was any space wasted. There were fresh flowers in a bowl on a Queen Anne desk. On the dresser was a collection of tiny bottles in pretty shapes and colors that could have no use at all. They, too, pleased her.

She stepped onto a rug in muted shades of rose and touched the curved back of a chair.

"I'm told you redecorated your room about three years ago," Reeve said casually. "It must be a comfort to know you have good taste."

Had she chosen the material for the soft, cushioned love seat herself? Brie ran her finger over it as if the feel would trigger some hint. Anything. From the window she could look down on Cordina as she must have done countless times before.

There were gardens, a roll of lawn, a jut of rock, the sea. Farther out was the city, houses and hills and green.

Though she couldn't see, she was sure children were still playing in the park near the fountain.

"Why am I blocking this out?" Brie demanded suddenly. When she turned around Reeve saw that the calm, reserved woman he'd brought upstairs had turned into an impassioned and desperate one. "Why do I block out what I want so badly to remember?"

"Maybe there are other things you're not ready to remember."

"I can't believe this." She flung down her purse on the love seat and began to pace, rubbing her hands against each other. "I can't bear having this wall between me and myself."

Fragility aside, he thought, there was a great deal of passion here. A man could find it difficult to overlook the combination and go about his business. "You'll have to be patient." And as he said it, he wondered if he was cautioning her or himself.

"Patient?" With a laugh she dragged a hand through her hair. "Why am I so sure that's something I'm not? I feel if I could push one brick, just one brick out of the wall, the rest would crumble away. But how?" She continued to move, quickly, with the kind of grace she'd been born with. "You could help me."

"Your family's here for that."

"No." The toss of her head was regal, and though

her voice was soft, it held command. "They know me, of course, but their feelings—and mine—will keep the wall up longer than I can stand. They look at me and hurt because I don't know them."

"But I don't know you."

"Exactly." She swept her hair away from her face with a gesture that seemed less impatient than habitual. "You'll be objective. Because you won't constantly try to protect my feelings you won't pull at them. Since you've already agreed to my father's request—haven't you?"

Reeve thought of his land. As he dipped his hands into his pockets, he frowned. "Yes."

"You've put yourself in the position of breathing over my shoulder," she continued smoothly, "and since you'll be there, you may as well be of some use to me."

He gave a half laugh. "My pleasure, Your Highness."

"Now I've annoyed you." With a shrug, she walked to him. "Well, I suppose we'll annoy each other a great deal before it's over. I'll be honest with you, not because I want your pity, but because I have to say it to someone. I feel so alone." Her voice wavered only slightly. The sun rushing through the windows betrayed her by revealing her pallor. "I have nothing I can see or touch that I know is mine. It isn't possible for me to look back a year and remember something funny or sad or sweet. I don't even know my full name."

He touched her. Perhaps he shouldn't have, but he couldn't stop. His fingers lifted to her face and just skimmed her cheek. "Her Serene Highness Gabriella Madeline Justine Bisset of Cordina."

"So much." She managed a smile, but her hand reached up to grip his tightly. The contact seemed a bit too natural for both of them, but neither broke it. "Brie seems easier. I can relax with Brie. Tell me, do you care for my family?"

"Yes."

"Then help me give them back the woman they need. Help me find her. In one week I've lost twenty-five years. I need to know why. You must understand that."

"I understand." But he told himself he shouldn't be touching her. "It doesn't mean I can help."

"But you can. You can because you have no need. Don't be patient with me, be harsh. Don't be kind, be hard."

He continued to hold her hand. "It might not be healthy for an American ex-cop to give a princess a hard time."

She laughed. It was the first time he'd heard it in ten years, yet he remembered. And he remembered, as she didn't, the swirl of the waltz they'd shared, the magic of moonlight. Staying wasn't wise, he knew. But he couldn't leave. Not quite yet.

Her fingers relaxed in his. "Do we still behead in

Cordina? Surely we have more civilized methods of dealing with rabble. Immunity." Suddenly she looked young and at ease. "I'll grant you immunity, Reeve MacGee. Hereby you have my permission to shout, probe, prod and be a general nuisance without fear of reprisal."

"You willing to put the royal seal on it?"

"After someone tells me where it is."

The intensity was gone. Pale and weary she might be, but her smile was lovely. He felt something else from her now. Hope and determination. He'd help her, Reeve thought. Later, perhaps, he'd ask himself why. "Your word's good enough."

"And yours. Thank you."

He brought the hand he still held to his lips. It was a gesture, he knew, she should be as accustomed to as breathing. Yet just as his lips brushed her knuckles he saw something flicker in her eyes. Princess or not, she was a woman. Reeve knew arousal when he saw it. Just as he knew it when he felt it. Cautious, he released her hand. The step back was for both of them.

"I'll leave you to rest. Your maid's name is Bernadette. Unless you want her sooner, she'll be in an hour before dinner."

Brie let her hand fall to her side as if it weren't part of her. "I appreciate what you're doing."

"You won't always." When he reached the door, he

judged the distance to be enough. Then he looked back, and she was still in front of the window. Light rioted in, flowing across her hair, shimmering over her skin. "Let it rest for today, Brie," he told her quietly. "Tomorrow we can start knocking at that brick."

Chapter 3

She hadn't meant to sleep but to think. Still, she felt herself drifting awake as groggy and disoriented as she'd been that first time in the hospital.

Gabriella, she told herself. Her name was Gabriella and she was lying in her room, on the soft blue-and-rose colored quilt that spread over her big carved oak bed. There was a breeze fluttering over her because she'd opened the windows herself when she'd explored her bedroom.

Her name was Gabriella and there was no reason to wake up afraid. Safe, she repeated over and over in her head until her muscles believed it and relaxed.

"So."

At the one indignant syllable, Brie sat up abruptly,

panicked. An old woman was seated neatly in a straight-backed chair across from the bed. Her hair was pulled back into a knot so tight that not a single wisp escaped. It was gray, stone gray, without a hint of softening white. Her face was like parchment, thin skinned, a bit yellowed and generously lined. Two small dark eyes peered out, and though her mouth was withered with age, it looked strong. She wore a dignified, no-nonsense black dress, sturdy black shoes and, quaintly, a cameo on a velvet ribbon around her neck.

Since Brie had no memory to rely on, she used instincts. Reeve had told her to observe without prejudice. It was advice she saw the wisdom in. There was no fear as she stared back at the old woman. Relaxing again, she remained sitting. "Hello."

"Fine thing," the old woman said in what rang to Brie as a Slavic accent. "You come home after giving me a week of worry and don't bother to see me."

"I'm sorry." The apology came out so naturally she smiled.

"They gave me this nonsense about your not remembering. Bah!" She lifted a hand and slapped it against the arm of the chair. "My Gabriella not remembering her own nanny."

Brie studied the woman but knew no sense of connection would come. It just wasn't time. "I don't remember," she said quietly. "I don't remember anything."

Nanny hadn't lived for seventy-three years, raised a nurseryful of children and buried one of her own without being prepared for any shock. After a moment's silence, she rose. Her face might be lined, her hands curled slightly with arthritis, but she pulled herself from the chair with the grace and ease of youth. As she stood over Brie's bed, the princess saw a small, birdlike woman in black with a stern face and rosary beads hanging from her belt.

"I am Carlotta Baryshnova, nanny to the Lady Honoria Bruebeck, your aunt, and Lady Elizabeth Bruebeck, your mother. When she became Princess Elizabeth of Cordina I came with her to be nanny to her children. I have diapered you, bandaged your knees and blown your nose. When you marry, I will do the same for your children."

"I see." Because the woman seemed more annoyed than upset, Brie smiled again. It occurred to her she had yet to see herself smile. She'd have to go back to the mirror again. "And was I a good child?"

"Hmph." The sound could have meant anything, but Brie caught a tiny hint of pleasure in it. "Sometimes worse, sometimes better than your brothers. And they were always a trial." Coming closer, she peered down at

Brie with the intensity of the nearsighted. "Not sleeping well," she said briskly. "No wonder. Tonight I'll bring you hot milk."

Brie angled her head. "Do I like it?"

"No. But you'll drink it. Now I'll run your bath. Too much excitement and too many doctors, that's what's wrong with you. I told that silly Bernadette I would see to your needs this evening. What have you done to your hands?" she demanded abruptly, and snatched one up. She began mumbling over it like an old hen over a backward chick. "Only a week away and you ruin your nails. Worse than a kitchen maid's. Chipped and broken, and with all the money you spend on manicures."

Brie sat still while Nanny fussed and complained. There was something, something in the feel of that dry, warm hand and scolding voice. Even as she tried to hold it, it faded. "I have manicures often?"

"Once a week." Nanny sniffed, but continued to grip Brie's fingers.

"It appears I need another one."

"You can have that stiff-lipped secretary of yours make an appointment. Your hair, too," Nanny said, scowling at it. "A fine thing for a princess to run around with chipped nails and flyaway hair. Fine thing," she continued, as she walked into an adjoining room. "Fine thing, indeed."

Brie rose and stripped. She felt no invasion of privacy at having the woman fuss and hover around during her bath. Even as she drew off her hose, the woman was there, bundling her into a short silk robe.

"Pin up your hair," Nanny said grumpily. "We'll do what we can with it after your bath." When she saw Brie's hesitation, she went to the dresser herself and opened a small enameled box. Hairpins were jumbled inside. "Here now." And her voice was more gentle. "Your hair is thick like your mother's. You need a lot of pins." She was nudging her along, clucking, into the room where water ran. Stopping a moment, Brie just looked.

There was a skylight, strategically placed so that the sun or rain or moonlight would be visible while looking up from the tub. The floor and walls were all tiled in white with flowering plants hanging everywhere in a room already steamy. Even with them, the tub dominated the room with its splash of rich, deep green. Its clover shape would accommodate three, she mused, and wondered if it ever had. Bemused, she watched the water pour out of a wide glistening faucet that turned it into a miniature waterfall.

She saw both the pristine and the passionate, and wondered if it reflected her. The scent rising out of the tub was the same that had been in the little glass bottle the prince had sent for that morning. Gabriella's scent, Brie reminded herself.

Letting the robe slip away, she lowered herself into the bath. It was easy to give herself to it as Nanny disappeared, muttering about laying out her clothes.

The water flowed hot around her. This was something she'd need, Brie discovered, if she were to make it through the evening ahead. She must have relaxed here countless times, looking up at the sky while thinking through what had to be done.

There would be dinner. In her mind she could imagine a complex, formal place setting. The silver, linen, crystal and china. It wasn't difficult for her to conjure up a menu and choose which wines with which course. That all seemed basic somehow, a knowledge that remained like knowing which articles of clothing to put on first. But she had no idea what pattern the china would have any more than she'd known what she'd find behind the wall of closets in her bedroom.

Struggling with impatience, she slipped lower in the water. Impatience, she'd discovered, was very much a part of her. Memory would come, Brie assured herself. And if it didn't come soon, naturally she'd find another way.

Reeve MacGee. Brie reached for the soap and a soft, oversized sponge. He might be her access to another way. Who was he? It was a relief to think of him rather than herself for a while. A former policeman, she remembered, and a friend of the family. Though not a close enough friend, Brie remembered, that he knew her well. He had his own life in America. Had she been there? He'd said she had.

She lay there, willing her mind to open. Only impressions came to her. Stately marble buildings and long formal dinners. And a river, a river with lush green grass on its banks and much boat traffic. It tired her, she discovered, to push herself to remember something even so unimportant. Still, she thought she'd been to Reeve's country.

Concentrate on him, Brie told herself. If he were to be any help to her she had to understand him. Good-looking, she thought, and very smooth on the outside. She wasn't so sure about what lay within. He seemed to her a man who would be ruthless and solitary, a man who did things in his own style. Good, she thought. That was precisely what she needed.

He had no reason, as her family did, to want to shield her. Nor did he have a reason, she added with a frown, to give her the help she wanted. Perhaps he'd agreed only to keep close to her so that he could do the job her father had commissioned him for. Bodyguard, she thought with annoyance. She wanted no one's shadow falling over hers.

And yet, Brie continued as she dipped the sponge into the water, isn't that what she'd asked for herself when she'd spoken to him? Because she'd felt...what, when she'd seen him standing in the hall? Relief. It shamed her to admit it. Her family had been there, concerned and loving, and yet she'd felt an overwhelming sense of relief seeing a stranger standing behind them.

Perhaps it was better that she'd forgotten herself. Brie threw down the sponge so that water splashed up and hit the side of the porcelain. How was she to know if she would like the woman she was? She might easily find herself to be someone cold, unfeeling, selfish. All she had discovered was that she was a woman who liked beautiful clothes and manicures. Perhaps she was just that shallow.

But they loved her. Brie picked up the sponge again to press it against her face. The water was hot and smelled like an expensive woman. The love she'd seen in her family's eyes had been real. Would they love her if she didn't deserve it? How long would it take to discover what depths there were in her?

Passions. She remembered the flare she'd felt when Reeve had kissed her hand. It had been sharp and raw and stunning. Didn't that mean she had normal feminine needs? But had she ever acted on them? With a half laugh, Brie lay her head back and closed her eyes. How many women could honestly say they didn't know if they were innocent or not?

Would he know? Would a man like Reeve sense such things about a woman? Sometimes when he looked at her Brie felt him reaching inside and finding nerves no stranger had a right to find. Now when she thought of him, she wondered what it would be like to have him touch her—really touch her. Fingertips against the skin, palm against flesh. She felt the arousal start deep, and let it work through her.

Was this a new experience? Brie wondered as she pressed a hand to her stomach. Had other men made her feel so…hungry? Were there other men who had sent her mind to wandering, imagining, dreaming? Perhaps she was a careless sort of woman who desired a man just because he was a man. Was she a woman a man would desire?

Rising from the tub, she let the water cascade from her. Reeve had been right about the possible advantages of her situation. She could watch and observe what reactions she brought to others. Tonight she would.

On the arm of her father, Brie walked down the long stairway. There'd be cocktails in the *petit salon,* he'd told her, but hadn't added he'd come for her because she wouldn't know the way. He did pause at the base of the stairs to kiss her hand. It was a gesture much like Reeve's, but brought her a smile rather than excitement.

"You look lovely, Brie."

"Thank you. But it would be difficult not to with the collection of clothes in my room."

He laughed and looked young. "You've often said clothes were your only vice."

"And are they?"

He heard the need behind the light question and kissed her hand again. "I've never been anything but proud of you." Tucking her hand through his arm again, he led her down the corridor.

Reeve noticed a certain tension between Alexander and Loubet, Armand's minister of state. It came out in politeness, the rigid sort. When Alexander takes the throne, Reeve thought dispassionately, Loubet would not be at his side.

Alexander interested Reeve. The young prince was so internal. Control didn't sit on him as easily as it did his father; he worked for it. Whatever simmered beneath was kept there, never permitted to boil—at least not in public. Unlike Bennett, Reeve thought, shifting his gaze to the other prince.

Bennett was relaxed in his chair, only half listening to

the conversation around him. He didn't seem to be compelled to analyze words and meanings as his brother did. His willingness to enjoy what came interested Reeve, as well.

As Gabriella did. Reeve had no way of knowing if the girl he'd met once had become an intense woman like her first brother, or a cheerful one like her second. Perhaps she was nothing like either. After two short conversations, he was as curious to find out as Brie herself.

Who was she? He asked of her the same question Brie had asked of him. Beautiful, yes. Classic looks and elegance hadn't been lost along with her memory. He sensed a steel will beneath them. She'd need it, he decided, if she was to discover herself.

Attraction. He certainly felt it for her. It wasn't anything like the dazzle he'd experienced ten years before. Now he saw her as a woman who struggled every moment not to lose control of a situation she couldn't even understand. If she could hang on while her world turned upside down around her, she wasn't a woman to underestimate.

Desire. He'd felt that, as well, each time he saw her. She had a way of looking at a man with those topaz eyes. Had she always? he wondered. Or was it simply now, when she was groping? A man had to be careful. She might look like a woman who could be touched, seduced, bedded, but she was and would always be a princess. Not the frothy fairy-tale sort, he thought, but flesh and blood.

When he turned and saw her, she seemed to be both.

Her head was lifted, as if she were walking into an arena rather than a salon. Clusters of pearls gleamed at her ears, at her throat, in her hair where it was swept back from her face. Her dress was the color of grapes just before they ripen. The silk and pearls suited her skin. Her stance suited her title. She didn't cling to her father, though Reeve thought she might have liked to cling to something. She was braced and ready. And, he thought with approval, she was watching.

"Your Highness."

Brie waited calmly while Loubet crossed the room and bowed. She saw a man, older than Reeve, younger than her father. His blond hair was just touched with gray, his face just touched with lines. He smelled distinguished, she thought, then smiled at how her mind worked. He walked with a slight stiffness of the left side, but his bow was very elegant and his smile charming.

"It's good to see you home."

She felt nothing when their hands touched, nothing when their eyes met. "Thank you."

"Monsieur Loubet and I had some business to attend

to this evening." Her father gave her the cue smoothly. "Unfortunately he won't be able to join us for dinner."

"Business and no pleasure, Monsieur Loubet," Brie said just as smoothly.

"It's a pleasure just to see you home safely, Your Highness."

Brie saw the quick glance that passed between the minister and her father. "Since the business pertained to me, perhaps you'll elaborate over drinks."

As she crossed the room, she caught Reeve's small nod of approval. Some of the knots in her stomach loosened. "Please, gentlemen, be comfortable." She indicated for everyone to sit. Everyone, she noted with a smile, but Bennett, who was already at his ease. "Do I have a favorite?" she asked him with a gesture toward the bar.

"Artesian water and lime," he said with a grin. "You've always said there's enough wine served at dinner without fuzzing your mind beforehand."

"Very sensible of me."

Reeve walked to the bar to see to her drink while Brie took a seat on one of the sofas. The men settled around her. Was her life so dominated by men? she wondered briefly, then took the glass and sipped. "Well, shall I tell you what I see?" Without waiting for a reply, she set down her glass and began. "I see Alexander is annoyed, and that my father is picking his way carefully, as a man through a minefield. I'm at the core of this."

"She should be left alone," Alexander stated suddenly. "It's family business."

"Your family's business remains Cordina's business, Your Highness." Loubet spoke gently but without, Brie thought, any affection. "Princess Gabriella's condition is a matter of concern both personally and for the government. I'm very much afraid that the matter of the temporary amnesia would be exploited by the world press if news of it leaks. We're just now settling our people down after the kidnapping. I wish only to give them and Her Serene Highness an opportunity to rest."

"Loubet is quite correct, Alexander." Armand spoke without gentleness, but Brie heard the affection.

"In theory." As he drank, Alexander shot Reeve a quietly resentful look. "But we already have outsiders involved. Gabriella needs rest and therapy. Whoever did this..." His fingers tightened on the facets of his glass. "Whoever did this will pay dearly."

"Alexander." Brie laid a hand on his in a gesture he recognized, but she didn't. "I have to remember what happened before anyone can pay."

"When you're ready, you will. In the meantime—"

"In the meantime," his father interrupted, "Brie must be protected in every possible way. And after consideration, I agree with Loubet that part of this protection should come from concealing the amnesia publicly. If the kidnappers knew you hadn't told us anything, they might feel compelled to silence you before you regained your memory."

Brie picked up her glass again, and though she sipped calmly, Reeve saw her eyes were anything but. "How can we conceal it?"

"If I may, Your Highness," Loubet began with a glance at Armand before he turned to Brie. "Until you're well, Your Highness, we think it best that you remain home, among those who can be trusted. It's a simple matter to postpone or cancel your outside commitments. The kidnapping, the strain and shock of it alone, will suffice without going further. The doctor who cared for you is your father's man. There's no fear that he'll leak any news of your condition except what we wish him to."

Brie set down her glass again. "No."

"I beg your—"

"No," she repeated very gently to Loubet, though her gaze shifted to her father. "I will not remain here like a prisoner. I believe I've been a prisoner quite long enough. If I have commitments, I'll meet them." She saw Bennett grin and lift his glass in salute.

"Your Highness, you must see how complicated and how dangerous this would be. If for no other reason than the police have yet to apprehend whoever kidnapped you."

"So, the solution is for me to remain closed up and closed in?" She shook her head. "I refuse."

"Gabriella, our duty is not always comfortable for us." Her father tapped the cigarette he'd lit during the conversation.

"Perhaps not. I can't speak from experience at the moment." She looked down at her hands, to the ring that was becoming familiar. "Whoever kidnapped me is still free. I mean to see they're not comfortable with that. Monsieur Loubet, you know me?"

"Your Highness, since you were a baby."

"Would you say I am a reasonably intelligent woman?"

Humor touched his eyes. "Far more than reasonably."

"I think then, with a bit of coaching, I could have my way, and you yours. The amnesia can be kept quiet if you feel that's best, but I won't hide in my rooms."

Armand started to speak, then sat back. A slight smile played on his lips. His daughter, he mused with approval, hadn't changed.

"Your Highness, I would personally be pleased to help you in any way, but—"

"Thank you, Loubet, but Mr. MacGee has already agreed to do so." Her voice was gracious and final.

"Whatever I need to know in order to be Princess Gabriella, he'll tell me."

There was quick resentment again from Alexander, speculation from Armand and barely controlled annoyance from Loubet. Reeve felt them all. "The princess and I have an arrangement of sorts." He sat comfortably, watching the reactions around him. "She feels that the company of a stranger might have certain advantages for her."

"We'll discuss this later." Armand rose, and though the words weren't abrupt, they were as final as his daughter's had been. "I regret your schedule doesn't permit you to dine, Loubet. We'll finish our business tomorrow morning."

"Yes, Your Highness."

Polite goodbyes, a distinguished exit. Brie looked after him thoughtfully. "He seems very sincere and dedicated. Do I like him?"

Her father smiled as he reached for her hand. "You never said specifically. He does his job well."

"And he's a dead bore," Bennett announced ungraciously as he rose. "Let's eat." He pulled Brie close by linking arms. "We're having the best of the best tonight in celebration. You can have a half-dozen raw oysters if you like."

"Raw? Do I like them?"

"Love them," he said blithely, and led her into dinner.

* * *

"It was…amusing to find Bennett enjoys a joke," Brie said some two hours later as she stepped onto a terrace with Reeve.

"Was it enlightening to learn you can take one?" He paused to cup his hand around his lighter. Smoke caught the breeze and billowed into the dark.

"Actually, yes. I've also learned I detest oysters and that I have a character that demands restitution. I'll get him back for tricking me into swallowing one of those things. In the meantime…" Turning, she leaned back against the strong stone banister. "I can see I've put you in a bit of an awkward position, Reeve. I didn't intend to, but now that I have, I'm afraid I don't intend to let you out."

"I can handle that for myself, when and if I choose."

"Yes." She smiled again. Then the smile became a laugh as she tossed her head back. Fear seemed so far away. Tension was so much simpler to deal with. "You could at that. Perhaps that's why I feel easy around you. Tonight I took your advice."

"Which was?"

"To observe. I have a good father. His position doesn't weigh lightly on him, nor does the strain of this past week. I see the servants treat him with great respect, but no fear, so I think he's just. Would you agree?"

The moonlight played tricks with her hair, making the pearls look like teardrops. "I would."

"Alexander is…what's the word I want?" With a shake of her head, she looked overhead to the sky. The long, pale line of her throat was exposed. "Driven, I suppose. He has the intensity of a much older man. I suppose he needs it. He hasn't decided to like you." When she shifted her head again, he found his eyes were on line with her lips.

"No."

"It doesn't bother you?"

"Not everyone's required to like me."

"I wish I had your confidence," she murmured. "In any case, I've added to whatever resentment he might feel toward you. Tonight when I said I wanted to walk outside and asked you to come with me, it annoyed him. His sense of family is very strong and very exclusive."

"You're his responsibility—in his opinion," Reeve added when she started to protest.

"His opinion will have to change. Bennett's different. He seems so carefree. Perhaps it's his age, or the fact that he's the younger son. Still, he watched me as though I might trip at any moment and need him to catch me. Loubet, what do you think of him?"

"I don't know him."

"Neither do I," she said wryly. "An opinion?"

"His position doesn't sit lightly on him, either."

It wasn't an evasion, Brie decided, any more than it was an answer. "You're a very elemental man, aren't you? Is it an American trait?"

"It's a matter of pushing away frills that just get in the way. You seem to be a very elemental woman."

"Do I?" She pursed her lips in thought. "It might be true, or it might be true now only out of necessity. I can't afford frills, can I?"

The strain of the evening had been more than she'd admit, Reeve observed as she turned again to rest her palms against the stone. She was tired, but he understood her reluctance to go in where she'd have nothing but her own questions for company.

"Brie, have you thought about taking a few days and going away?" She lifted her head. Sensing the anger in her, he laid a hand on her shoulder. "Not running away, getting away. It's human."

"I can't afford to be human until I know who I am."

"Your doctor said the amnesia's temporary."

"What's temporary?" she demanded. "A week, month, year? Not good enough, Reeve. I won't just sit and wait for things to come to me. In the hospital I had dreams." She closed her eyes a moment, breathed deep and continued. "In the dreams I was awake, but not awake. I couldn't move. It was dark and I couldn't make myself move. Voices. I could hear voices, and I'd struggle and struggle to understand them, recognize them, but I'm afraid. In the dream I'm terrified, and when I wake, I'm terrified."

He drew in sharply on his cigarette. She said it without any emotion, and the lack of feeling said a great deal. "You were drugged."

Very slowly, she turned toward him again. In the shadowed light her eyes were very clear. "How do you know?"

"The doctors had to pump you. It's the opinion from the state you were in that you were kept drugged. Even when your memory comes back, Brie, you may not be able to pinpoint anything that happened during the week you were held. That's something you'd better face now."

"Yes, I will." She pressed her lips together until she was certain her voice would be strong. "I will remember. How much more do you know?"

"Not a great deal."

"Out with it."

He flipped his cigarette over the banister and into the void. "All right, then. You were abducted sometime Sunday. No one knows the exact time, as you were out driving alone. Sunday evening a call came in to Alexander."

"Alex?"

"Yes, he usually works on Sunday evenings in his office. He has a separate line there as all of you do in your own quarters. The call was brief. It said simply that you'd been taken and would be held until the ransom demands were met. No demands were made at that time."

And where had she been held? Dark. All she could be certain of was dark. "What did Alex do?"

"He went directly to your father. You were searched for. Monday morning your car was found on a lane about forty miles from town. There's a plot of land out there you own. It seems you have a habit of driving out there just to be alone and poke around. Monday afternoon, the first ransom demand was made. That was for money. There was no question about it being paid, of course, but before the arrangement could be made, another call came. This one demanded the release of four prisoners in exchange for you."

"And that complicated things."

"Two of them are set for execution. Espionage," he added when she remained silent. "It took the matter out of your father's hands. Money was one thing, releasing prisoners another. Negotiations were well under way when you were found on the side of the road."

"I'll go back there," Brie mused. "To the place my car was found and to the place I was found."

"Not right away. I agreed to help you, Brie, but in my way."

Her eyes narrowed ever so slightly. "Which is?"

"My way," he said simply. "When I think you're strong enough, I'll take you. Until then, we move slow."

"If I don't agree?"

"Your father might just take Loubet's plan more seriously."

"And I'd go nowhere."

"That's right."

"I knew you wouldn't be an easy man, Reeve." She walked a few feet away, into a stream of moonlight. "I haven't much choice. I don't like that. Choice seems to me to be the most essential freedom. I keep wondering when I'll have mine back. Tomorrow, after I meet with my secretary…"

"Smithers," Reeve supplied. "Janet Smithers."

"What a prim name," Brie observed. "I'll go over my schedule with Janet Smithers in the morning. Then I'd like to go over it with you. Whatever it is I'm committed to do, I want to do. Even if it's spending hours shopping or sitting in a beauty parlor."

"Is that how you think you spend your time?"

"It's a possibility. I'm rich, aren't I?"

"Yes."

"Well, then…" With a shrug, she trailed off. "Tonight,

before dinner, I lay in the bath and wondered. Actually, I thought of you and wondered."

Very slowly he dipped his hands in his pockets. "Did you?"

"I tried to analyze you. In some ways I could and others not. If I had a great deal of experience with men, it's forgotten along with everything else, you see." She felt no embarrassment as she walked to him again. "I wondered if I were to kiss you, be held by you, if I'd see that part of me."

Rocking back on his heels, he studied her blandly. "Just part of the job, Your Highness?"

Annoyance flickered in her eyes. "I don't care how you look at it."

"Maybe I do."

"Do you find me unattractive?"

He saw the way her lip thrust forward so slightly in a pout as she asked. She seemed a woman accustomed to flowery, imaginative compliments. She wouldn't get them from him. "Not unattractive."

She wondered why it sounded almost like an insult. "Well, then, do you have a woman you're committed to? Would you feel dishonest if you kissed me?"

He made no move toward her, and the bland smile remained. "I've no commitments, Your Highness."

"Why are you calling me that now?" she demanded. "Is it only to annoy me?"

"Yes."

She started to become angry, then ended up laughing. "It works."

"It's late." He took her hand in a friendly manner. "Let me take you up."

"You don't find me unattractive." She strolled along with him, but at her own pace. "You have no allegiances. Why won't you kiss me then and help? You did agree to help."

He stopped and looked down at her. The top of her head came to his chin. With her chin tilted back, she looked eye to eye with him. "I told your father I'd keep you out of trouble."

"You told me you'd help me find out who I am. But perhaps your word means nothing," she said lightly. "Or perhaps you're a man who doesn't enjoy kissing a woman."

She'd taken only two steps, when he caught her arm. "You don't pull any punches, do you?"

She smiled. "Apparently."

He nodded, then held her close in his arms. "Neither do I."

He touched his lips to hers with every intention of keeping the kiss dispassionate, neutral. Though he understood her reasons, her needs, he also understood she'd goaded him into doing something he was better off avoiding. Hadn't he wondered what that soft, curving mouth would taste like? Hadn't he imagined how that slim, fragile body would feel in his arms? But he'd agreed to do a job. He'd never taken any job lightly.

So he touched his lips to hers, intending on keeping the kiss neutral. Neutrality lasted no more than an instant.

She was soft, frail, sweet. He had to protect her. She was warm, tempting, arousing. He had to take her. Her eyes were open, just. He could see the glimmer of gold through the thick lashes as he slid his hand up to cup her neck. And he could feel, as the kiss deepened beyond intention, her unhesitating, unapologetic response.

Their tongues met, skimmed, then lingered, drawing out flavors. She wound her arms invitingly around him so that her body pressed without restriction to his. The scent she wore was darker then the sky, deeper than the mixed fragrance of night blossoms that rose from the gardens below. Moonlight splashed over him and onto her. He could almost believe in fairy tales again.

She thought she'd known what to expect. Somewhere inside her was the memory of what a kiss was, just as she knew what food, what drink were. And yet, with his mouth on hers, her mind, her emotions were a clean slate. He wrote on them what he chose.

If her blood had run hot before, she didn't remember it. If her head had swum, she had no recollection. Everything was fresh, new, exciting. And yet...and yet there was a depth here, a primitive need that came without surprise.

Yearning, dreaming, longing. She may have done so before. Aching, needing, wanting. She might not remember, but she understood. It was him, holding her close—him, rushing kisses over her face—him, breathing her name onto her lips, that brought these things all home again.

But had there been others? Who? How many? Had she stood in the moonlight wrapped in strong arms before? Had she given herself so unhesitatingly to passion before? Had it meant nothing to her, or everything? Shaken, she drew away. What kind of woman gave a man her soul before she knew him? Or even herself?

"Reeve." She stepped back carefully. Doubts dragged at her. "I'm not sure I understand any better."

He'd felt it from her. Complete, unrestricted passion. Even as he wanted to reach out for it again, the same reasoning came to him. How many others? Unreasonably he wanted that heat, that desire to be his alone. He offered his hand but kept his distance. It wasn't a feeling he welcomed.

"We'd both better sleep on it."

Chapter 4

She felt like an imposter. Brie was in her tidy no-frills all-elegance office only because Reeve had taken her there. She'd been grateful when he'd knocked on her sitting room door at eight with a simple, "Are you ready?" and nothing else. The prospect of having to ask one of the palace staff to show her the way hadn't appealed. On her first full day back, Brie didn't want to have to start off dealing with expectations and curiosity. With him, she didn't have to apologize, fumble or explain.

Reeve was here, Brie told herself, to do exactly what he was doing: guide her discreetly along. As long as she remembered that, and not the moments they'd spent on the terrace the night before, she'd be fine. She'd have felt better if she hadn't woken up thinking of them.

After a short, nearly silent walk through the corridors, where Brie had felt all the strain on her side and none on Reeve's, he'd shown her to the third-floor corner room in the east wing.

Once there, she toured it slowly. The room wasn't large, but it was all business. Good light, a practical set-up, privacy. The furniture might have been exquisite, but it wasn't frivolous. That relieved her.

The capable mahogany desk that stood in the center was orderly. The colors were subdued, pastels again, she noted, brushing past the two chairs with their intricate Oriental upholstery and ebony wood. Again, flowers were fresh and plentiful—pink roses bursting up in a Sevres vase, white carnations delicate in Wedgwood. She pulled out a bud and twirled it by its stem as she turned back to Reeve.

"So I work here." She saw the thick leather book on the desk, but only touched it. Would she open it to find her days filled with lunches, teas, fittings, shopping? And if she did, could she face it? "What work do I do?"

It was a challenge. It was a plea. Both were directed to him.

He'd done his homework. While Brie had slept the afternoon before, Reeve had gone through her files, her appointment book, even her diary. There was little of Her

Serene Highness Gabriella de Cordina he didn't know. But Brie Bisset was a bit more internal.

He'd spent an hour with her secretary and another with the palace manager. There had been a brief, cautious interview with her former nanny in which he'd had to gradually chip away at a protective instinct that spanned generations. The picture he gained made Princess Gabriella more complex, and Brie Bisset more intriguing than ever.

He'd decided to help her because she needed help, but nothing was ever that simple. The puzzle of her kidnapping nagged at him, prodded, taunted. On the surface, it seemed as though her father was leaving the investigation to the police and going about his business. Reeve rarely believed what was on the surface. If Armand was playing a chess game with him as queen's knight, he'd play along, and make some moves of his own. It hadn't taken Reeve long to discover that royalty was insular, private and closemouthed. So much better the challenge. He wanted to put the pieces of the kidnapping together, but to do so, he had to put the pieces of Gabriella together first.

From her description of her family the day before, Reeve had thought her perceptive. Her impression of herself, however, was far from accurate. Or perhaps it was the fear of herself, Reeve reflected. For a moment, he speculated on what it would be like to wake up one morning with no past, no ties, no sense of self. Paralyzing. Then he quickly dismissed the idea. The more sympathetic he was toward her, the more difficult his job.

"You're involved in a number of projects," he said simply, and stepped forward to the desk. "Some you'd term day-to-day duties, and others official."

It came back to her then, hard, just what had passed between them the night before. Being moved, being driven. Had any other man made her feel like that before? She didn't step back, but she braced herself. Emotions, whatever they might be, couldn't be allowed to interfere with what she had to do.

"Projects?" she repeated smoothly. "Other than having my nails painted?"

"You're a bit hard on Gabriella, aren't you?" Reeve murmured. He dropped his hand on hers, on the leather book. For five humming seconds they stood just so.

"Perhaps. But I have to know her to understand her. At this point, she's more a stranger to me than you are."

Sympathy rose up again. Whatever his wish, he couldn't deny it completely. The hand under his was firm; her voice was strong, but in her eyes he saw the self-doubt, the confusion and the need. "Sit down, Brie."

The gentleness of his voice had her hesitating. When a man could speak like that, what woman was safe?

Slowly she withdrew her hand from his and chose one of the trim upholstered chairs. "Very well. This is to be lesson one?"

"If you like." He sat on the edge of the desk so that there was a comfortable distance between them, and so that he could look fully into her face. "Tell me what you think of when you think of a princess."

"Are you playing analyst?"

He crossed his ankles. "It's a simple question. You can make the answer as simple as you like."

She smiled and seemed to relax with it. "Prince Charming, fairy godmothers, glass slippers." She brushed the rose petals idly against her cheek and looked beyond him to a sunbeam that shot onto the floor. "Footmen in dashing uniforms, carriages with white satin seats, pretty silver crowns, floaty dresses. Crowds of people.... Crowds of people," she repeated, and her eyes focused on the stream of sunlight, "cheering below the window. The sun's in your eyes so that it's difficult to see, but you hear. You wave. There's the smell of roses, strong. A sea of people with their voices rising up and up so that they wash over you. Lovely, sweet, demanding." She fell silent, then dropped the rose in her lap.

Her hand had trembled; he'd seen it the instant before she'd dropped the flower. "Is that your imagination, or do you remember that?"

"I…" How could she explain? She could still smell the roses, hear the cheers, but she couldn't remember. She could feel the way the sun made her eyes sting, but she couldn't put herself at the window. "Impressions only," she told him after a moment. "They come and go. They never stay."

"Don't push it."

Her head whipped around. "I want—"

"I know what you want." His voice was calm, even careless. Annoyance flashed in her eyes. It was something he knew how to deal with. He picked up the appointment book but didn't open it. "I'll give you an average day in the life of Her Serene Highness Gabriella de Cordina."

"And how do you know?"

Reeve tested the weight of the book as he watched her. "It's my job to know. You rise at seven-thirty and breakfast in your room. From eight-thirty to nine you meet with the palace manager."

"Régisseur." She blinked, then her brows knit. "That's the French. He would be called *régisseur,* not manager."

Reeve made no comment while she continued to frown, struggling to remember why the term was so familiar to her. "You decide on the day's menus. If there's no official dinner, you normally plan the main meal for midday. This was a duty you assumed when your mother died."

"I see." She waited for the grief. Longed for it. She felt nothing. "Go on."

"From nine to ten-thirty you're here in your office with your secretary, handling official correspondence. Generally, you'll dictate to her how to answer, then sign the letters yourself once they're in order."

"How long has she been with me?" Brie asked abruptly. "This Janet Smithers?"

"A little under a year. Your former secretary had her first child and retired."

"Am I…" Groping for the word, she wiggled her fingers. "Do I have a satisfactory relationship with her?"

Reeve tilted his head. "No one told me of any complaint."

Frustrated, Brie shook her head. How could she explain to a man that she wanted to know how she and her secretary were woman to woman? How could she explain that she wondered if she had any close female friends, any woman that would break the circle of men she seemed to be surrounded with? Perhaps this was one more thing she'd have to determine for herself. "Please, continue."

"If there's time, you take care of any personal correspondence, as well, during the morning session. Otherwise, you leave that for the evening."

It seemed tedious, she mused, then thought that obligations often were. "What is 'official correspondence'?"

"You're the president for The Aid to Handicapped Children Organization. The AHC is Cordina's largest charity. You're also a spokesperson for the International Red Cross. In addition you're deeply involved with the Fine Arts Center, which was built in your mother's name. It falls to you to handle correspondence from the wives of heads of state, to head or serve on various committees, to accept or decline invitations and to entertain during state functions. Politics and government are your father's province, and to some extent, Alexander's."

"So I confine myself to more—feminine duties?"

She saw the grin, fast, appealing, easy. "I wouldn't put a label on it after looking at your schedule, Brie."

"Which so far," she pointed out, "consists of answering letters."

"Three days a week you go to the headquarters of the AHC. Personally, I wouldn't want to handle the influx of paperwork. You've been bucking the National Council for eighteen months on an increase in budget for the Fine Arts Center. Last year you toured fifteen countries for the Red Cross and spent ten days in Ethiopia. There

was a ten-page spread in *World* magazine. I'll see that
you get a copy."

She picked up the rose again, running her finger over
the petals as she rose to pace. "But am I clever at it?" she
demanded. "Do I know what I'm doing, or am I simply
there as some kind of figurehead?"

Reeve drew out a cigarette. "Both. A beautiful young
princess draws attention, press, funds and interest. A
clever young woman uses that and her brain to get what
she's after. According to your diary—"

"You've read my diary?"

He lifted a brow, studying the combination of outrage
and embarrassment on her face. She'd have no idea, he
mused, if there was any need for the embarrassment.
"You've asked me to help you," he reminded her. "I can't
help you unless I know you. But relax—" Reeve lit the
cigarette with a careless flick of his lighter "—you're
very discreet, Gabriella, even in what you write in your
personal papers."

There was no use squirming, she told herself. He'd
very probably enjoy it. "You were saying?"

"According to your diary, the traveling is wearing.
You've never been particularly fond of it, but you do it,
year in and year out, because it's necessary. Funds must
be raised, functions attended. You work, Gabriella. I
promise you."

"I'll have to take your word for it." She slipped the rose back into the vase. "And I want to begin. First, if I'm to keep the loss of memory discreet, I need the names of people I should know." Skirting around the desk, she took her seat and picked up a pen. "You'll give me what you know. Then I'll call Janet Smithers. Do I have appointments today?"

"One o'clock at the AHC Center."

"Very well. I've a lot to learn before one."

By the time Reeve left her with her secretary, he'd given Brie more than fifty names, with descriptions and explanations. He'd consider it a minor miracle if she retained half of them.

If he'd had a choice, Reeve would have gotten in his car and driven. Toward the sea, toward the mountains—it didn't matter. Palaces, no matter how spacious, how beautiful, how historically fascinating, were still walls and ceilings and floors. He wanted the sky around him.

Only briefly, Reeve paused at a window to look out before he climbed to the fourth floor and Prince Armand's office. A cop's work, he thought with some impatience. Legwork and paperwork. He was still a long way from escaping it.

He was admitted immediately, to find the prince pouring coffee. The room was twice the size of Brie's, much more ornate and rigidly masculine. The molding on the lofted ceiling might have been intricately carved and gilded, but the chairs were wide, the desk oak and solid. Armand had the windows open, so that the light spilled across the huge red carpet.

"Loubet has just left," Armand said without preliminary. "You've seen the paper?"

"Yes." Reeve accepted the coffee but didn't sit, as the prince remained standing. He knew when to reject protocol and when to bow to it. "It appears there's relief that Her Highness is back safely and a lot of speculation on the kidnapping itself. It's to be expected."

"And a great deal of criticism of Cordina's police department," Armand added, then shrugged. "That, too, is to be expected. I feel so myself, but, then, they have next to nothing to go on."

Reeve inclined his head, coolly. "Don't they?"

Their look held, each measuring the other. "The police have their duty, I mine and you yours. You've been with Gabriella this morning?"

"Yes."

"Sit." With an impatient gesture he motioned toward a chair. Protocol be damned, he wasn't ready to sit himself. "How is she?"

Reeve took a seat and watched the prince walk around the room with the same nervous grace his daughter had.

"Physically, I'd say she's bouncing back fast. Emotionally, she's holding on because she's determined to. Her secretary's briefing her on names and faces at the moment. She intends to keep her schedule, starting today."

Armand drank half his coffee, then set the cup down. He'd already had too much that morning. "And you'll go with her?"

Reeve sipped his coffee. It was dark and rich and hot. "I'll go with her."

"It's difficult—" Armand broke off, struggling with some emotion. Anger, sorrow, frustration? Reeve couldn't be quite sure. "It's difficult," he repeated, but with perfect calm, "to stand back and do little, give little. You came at my request. You stayed at my request. And now I find myself jealous that you have my daughter's trust."

"'Trust' might be a bit premature. She considers me useful at the moment." He heard the annoyance in his voice and carefully smoothed it over. "I can give her information about herself without drawing on her emotions."

"Like her mother, she has many of them. When she loves, she loves completely. That in itself is a treasure."

Armand let his coffee cool as he walked around to sit at his desk. It was an official move, of that Reeve was certain. Imperceptibly he came to attention. "Last evening Bennett pointed out to me that I may have put you in an awkward position."

Reeve sipped his coffee, outwardly relaxed, inwardly waiting. "In what way?"

"You'll be at Gabriella's side, privately and publicly. Being who she is, Brie is photographed often. Her life is a subject for discussion." The prince picked up a smooth white rock that sat on his desk. It just fitted in the palm of his hand; it was a rock his wife had found years before on a rocky beach. "With my thoughts centered around Gabriella's safety and her recovery, I hadn't considered the implications of your presence."

"As to my…place in Gabriella's life?"

Armand's lips curved. "It's a relief not to have to explain everything with delicacy. Bennett's young, and his own affairs are lovingly described in the international press." There seemed to be a mixture of pride and annoyance. A parent's fate, Reeve thought with some amusement. He'd seen it in his father often enough. "Perhaps that's why this occurred to him first."

"I'm here for Her Highness's security," Reeve commented. "It seems simple enough."

"For the ruler of Cordina to have asked a former policeman, an American policeman, to guard his daughter, is not simple. It would, perhaps rightly, be considered an insult. We're a small country, Reeve, but pride is no small thing."

Reeve sat silently a moment, weighing, considering. "Do you want me to leave?"

"No."

Relief. It shouldn't be what he was feeling, certainly not so intensely. But his hand on the cup relaxed. "I can't change my nationality, Armand."

"No." His answer was just as brief. He passed the rock into his other hand. "It would be possible, however, to change your position in such a way that would allow you to remain close to Gabriella without causing the wrong kind of speculation."

This time it was Reeve who smiled. "As a suitor?"

"Again you make it easy for me." Armand sat back, studying the son of his friend. Under less complicated circumstances, he might have approved of a match between Reeve and his daughter. He couldn't deny he had hoped Brie would marry before this, and that he'd purposely tossed her together with members of British royalty and gentry, eligible men of the French aristocracy. Still, the MacGees had an impressive lineage and a flawless reputation. He wouldn't have been displeased if what he was now proposing hypothetically were fact.

"I would, however, take it one step closer than a suitor. If you have no objections, I'd like to announce your engagement to Gabriella." He waited for some sign, some gesture or expression. Reeve gave him nothing more than what seemed to be polite interest. Armand rubbed a thumb over the rock. He could respect a man who could keep his thoughts to himself.

"As her fiancé," he continued, "you can be by her side without raising any questions."

"The question might arise as to how I became Her Highness's fiancé after being in Cordina only a few days."

Armand nodded, liking the clean, emotionless response. "My long association with your father makes this more than plausible. Brie was in your country only last year. It could be said that you developed your relationship then."

Reeve drew out a cigarette. He found he needed one. "Engagements have a habit of leading to marriage."

"Proper ones, yes." Armand set the stone back on his desk and folded his hands. "This, of course, is only one for our convenience. When the need is over, we'll announce that you and Gabriella have had a change of heart. The engagement will be broken and you'll each go your own way. The press will enjoy the melodrama and no harm will be done."

The princess and the farmer, Reeve thought, and grinned. It might be an interesting game at that. Before it was over, there might be a few moments to remember. "Even if I agree, there's another player involved."

"Gabriella will do what's best for herself and her country." He spoke simply, as a man who knows his own power. "The choice is yours, not hers."

A lack of choice. Hadn't she said that was what she resented most? There was more to being royal than the pretty silver crown and glass slipper. Reeve blew out a stream of smoke. He might sympathize, but it wouldn't stop him from making this choice for her. "I can understand your reasons. We'll play it your way, Armand."

The prince rose. "I'll speak to Gabriella."

Reeve hadn't thought she'd be pleased. When it came down to it, he didn't want her to be. It was easier on him when she was a bit prickly, a little icy. It was the lost, vulnerable look that undid him.

When Brie swept out of the palace a few minutes before one, he wasn't disappointed. She'd thrown on a jacket, the same dark, rich suede as her skirt. Her hair fell free down the back and caught every color of the sun. Her eyes, when she tossed her head back and aimed them at him, were gold, glorious and molten. A creature of the light, he thought as he lounged against the car. She didn't belong behind castle walls, but under the sky.

Reeve gave her a small bow as he opened the door for her. Brie sent him one long smoldering look. "You stabbed me in the back." She dropped into the front seat and stared straight ahead.

Reeve jingled the keys in his pocket as he crossed over to the driver's side. He could handle it delicately… or he could handle it as he chose. "Something wrong, darling?" he asked her when he settled beside her.

"You're joking?" She looked at him again, hard and full. "You dare?"

He took her hand, holding it though she gave it a good, hard jerk. "Gabriella, some things are best taken lightly."

"This farce. This deceit!" Abruptly, and with finesse, she went off in a stream of rapid, indignant French he could only partially follow. The tone, however, was crystal clear. "First I have to accept you as a bodyguard," she continued, reverting to English without a pause. "So that whenever I turn you'll be there, hovering. Now this pretense that we're to be married. And for what?" she demanded. "So that it won't be known that my father has engaged a bodyguard who isn't Cordinian or French. So that I may be seen constantly with a man without damaging my reputation. Hah!" In a bad tempered and undeniably regal gesture, she flung out a hand. "It's *my* reputation."

"There's always mine," he said coolly.

With that she turned to him, giving him a haughty stare, first down, then up. "I believe it's safe to say you have one already. And it doesn't concern me," she added before he could speak.

"As my fiancée, it certainly should." Reeve started the engine and began the leisurely drive down.

"It's a ridiculous charade."

"Agreed."

That stopped her. She had opened her mouth to continue to rage, then closed it again with a nearly audible snap. "You find it ridiculous to be engaged to me?"

"Absolutely."

She discovered something else about herself. She had a healthy supply of vanity. "Why?"

"I generally don't get engaged to women I barely know. Then, too, I'd think twice about hooking up with someone who was willful, selfish and bad tempered."

Her chin came up. From out of her bag she grabbed a pair of tinted glasses and stuck them on her nose. "Then you're fortunate it's only a pretense, aren't you?"

"Yes."

She snapped her bag closed. "And of short duration."

He didn't grin. A man only takes a certain amount of risks in one day. "The shorter the better."

"I'll do my best to accommodate you." She took the rest of the journey in simmering silence.

It was a short one, but she wasn't grateful for it. Having something, someone, specific to direct her anger at helped ease the fear of facing people who were only names to her. She would have liked more time to prepare.

The building that housed the headquarters for the Aid to Handicapped Children Organization was old and distinguished. It had once been the home of her great-grandmother, the thin, efficient Janet Smithers had told her.

Brie stepped from the car with practiced ease. Her stomach muscles were jumping. As she walked to the entrance, she went over the floor plan in her mind. She wouldn't have reached for Reeve's hand, but when his closed over hers, she didn't pull away. Sometimes it was necessary, even preferable, to hold hands with the devil.

She stepped inside, into a cool white hall. Immediately a woman who sat at a desk just beyond the entrance rose and curtsied. "Your Highness. It's so good to see you safe."

"Thank you, Claudia." The hesitation on the name was so brief Reeve hardly noticed it himself.

"We didn't expect you, Your Highness. After what—what happened." Her voice faltered. Her eyes filled.

Compassion moved Brie, before instinct, before politics. She held out both hands. "I'm fine, Claudia. Anxious to get to work." There was a warmth here, a bond she hadn't felt with her personal secretary. Still, there could be no pursuing it until she understood it. "This is Mr. MacGee. He's...staying with us. Claudia's been with AHC for nearly ten years, Reeve." Brie gave him the information he'd given her only that morning. "I believe she could run the organization single-handed. Tell me, Claudia, have you left anything for me to do?"

"There's the ball, Your Highness. As usual, there are complications."

The Annual Charity Ball, Brie recited to herself. A tradition in Cordina and the biggest fundraiser for the AHC. She, as president, would organize. As princess she would hostess. It drew the rich, the famous and the important to Cordina every spring. "It wouldn't be the ball without complications. I'll get to work, then. Come on, Reeve, we'll see how useful you can be."

Past the first hurdle, she went up the stairs, down the hall and into the second room on the right.

"Well done," Reeve told her as she closed the door.

"I keep hoping…" With a shrug, she let the thought go. She kept hoping that someone would trigger something, would trip the first lock on her memory so that remembrances would come through. Briskly she moved over and drew the curtains.

The room wasn't as elegant as her personal office. There was a row of file cabinets along one wall, metal and businesslike. Though the desk was ornate, made of beautiful cherry, it was covered with files and notes and papers. Going over, she sat down and picked one up. It was a note concerning a donation to the pediatric ward of the hospital in her handwriting.

Odd to see it, she mused. Earlier she'd tested herself by simply picking up a pen and writing out her name, just to see her signature. The writing was big, looping, just bordering on the undisciplined, and very distinctive. Brie set down the note and wondered where to begin.

"I'll see about some coffee," Reeve suggested.

"And some cakes or cookies," Brie said absently as she began to sort through the papers on her desk. "I missed lunch." Looking up, she lifted a brow. "I was too angry to eat, but it appears I'm going to need something before this is done."

"Hamburger?"

"Cheeseburger, no onions." Then she grinned because it had come out so naturally. "I like them well done." She could almost, almost picture herself sitting at that desk with a harried, impromptu lunch while she made calls and signed papers. With a burst of enthusiasm, she began to organize.

She was good at it. It was thrilling to discover she had a talent. Within two hours she'd assessed the situation in her office and had begun, slowly, systematically to cope with details, problems and decisions. It came naturally, as dressing, eating, walking came. She had only to think of the angles, consider them and work her way through. At the end of her two hours, her confidence was strong and her mood high. When she left the office her desk was still cluttered. But it was her clutter now—she understood it.

"It felt good," she said to Reeve when she settled in the car again. "So good. You'll think I'm foolish."

"Not at all." He sat beside her but didn't reach for the key just yet. "You accomplished a hell of a lot in a couple of hours, Brie. As a cop, I know just how frustrating and boring paperwork can be."

"But when it does something, it's worth the headache, isn't it? AHC is a good organization. It doesn't just preach. It helps. All that equipment in the pediatric ward, the new wing. The wheelchairs, walkers, hearing aids, tutors. They cost money, and we get the money." She glanced down at the glitter of diamonds and sapphires on her finger. "It makes me feel justified."

"Do you need to be?"

"Yes. Just because I was born to something doesn't mean I don't have to earn the right to it. Especially now when…"

"You can't remember being born to it."

"I don't know how I felt before," she murmured, staring down at the elegant little leather purse she carried. "I only know how I feel now. I've been given a title, but it doesn't come without a price, that I know."

He started the car. "You learn fast."

"I have to." Weariness was there, but she didn't relax. She couldn't. "Reeve, I don't want to go back just yet. Can we drive? Anywhere, it doesn't matter. I just need to be out."

"All right." He understood the need to be away from walls, from restrictions. He'd grown up with them, as well. He'd rebelled against them, as well. Without thinking, he headed toward the sea.

There were places just outside the capital where the road stretched and curved along the seawall. There were places before Cordina's port, Lebarre, where the land was wild and free and open. Reeve pulled up beside a clump of pitted rocks where the trees grew slanted, leaning away from the wind.

Brie got out of the car and drank the scene in. Somehow she knew the scent and taste of the sea. She couldn't be certain she'd been to this spot before, yet it soothed her. Letting the need to know slip away, she walked toward the old, sturdy seawall.

Tiny springy purple flowers crowded their way up through the cracks, determined to have the sun. She reached to touch one but didn't pick it. It would die too quickly. Unmindful of her skirt, she sat on the wall and looked down.

The sea was single-mindedly blue. If it had had its

way, it would have consumed the land. The wall prevented that, but didn't tame it. Farther out she could see ships, big freighters that were on their way to or from the port, sleek sailing boats with their canvas taut. She thought her hands had known the feel of rope, her body the sway of the sea. Perhaps soon she'd test it.

"Some things are comfortable right away. Familiar, I mean. This is one of them."

"You couldn't grow up near the sea and not find spots like this." The wind whipped her hair back, tossing it up and away from her face. Its color was nearly gold in this light, with small flames licking through it. He sat beside her, but not too close.

"I think I'd come to a place like this, just to breathe when the protocol became too tedious to stand." She sighed, closing her eyes as she lifted her face to the wind. "I wonder if I always felt that way."

"You could ask your father."

She lowered her head. When their eyes met, he saw the weariness she'd been so careful to hide. She wasn't back on full power yet, he reflected. And he wasn't immune to vulnerability.

"It's difficult." Anger and annoyance, strain and tension were forgotten as she felt herself drawn to him again. She could talk to him, say whatever was on her mind, without consequences. "I don't want to hurt him.

I feel such intense love, such fierce protection from him it disturbs me. I know he's waiting for me to remember everything."

"Aren't you?"

She looked back out to sea, silent.

"Brie, don't you want to remember?"

It was the sea she continued to look at, not him. "Part of me does—desperately. And then another part pushes away, as if it's all just too much. If I remember the good, won't I remember the bad?"

"You're not a coward."

"I wonder. Reeve, I remember running. The rain, the wind. I remember running until I thought I'd die from it. Most of all, I remember the fear, a fear so great that I would have preferred dying to stopping. I'm not sure that part of me will allow the memory to come back."

He understood what she described. The knowledge ate at him, something he couldn't allow. Something he couldn't prevent. "When you're strong enough, you won't give yourself a choice."

"Something inside of me is afraid of that, too. At a time like this—" she shook her hair back and enjoyed the feel of it lifting off her neck "—it would be so easy to relax and let it go, to just allow things to happen. If I weren't what I am I could do that. No one would care."

"You are what you are."

"You don't dream?" she asked with a half smile. "You don't ever ask yourself, what if? I could sit here now and pretend I had a cottage in the hills and a garden. Perhaps my husband's a farmer and I'm carrying our first child. Life is simple and very sweet."

"And the woman in the cottage could pretend she was a princess who lived in a palace." He touched a strand of her hair that danced in the wind. "Life's full of dreams, Brie. It's never simple, but it can be sweet."

"What do you dream?"

He curled her hair around the tip of his finger, then set it free. "Of tilling my own land, watching my crops grow. Being away from the streets."

"You have land in America? A farm?"

"Yeah." He thought of it waiting for him. Next year, he promised himself. He'd waited this long.

"But I thought you were a policeman — no, a detective now, working for yourself. A kind of adventurer."

He laughed at the term, not bitter, just amused. "People outside the business tend to think of dark alleys and forget the paperwork."

"But you've seen the dark alleys."

He gave her a look, one hard and calm enough to make her swallow. "I've seen them, maybe too many of them."

She thought she understood. She knew, without knowing, that she'd traveled a dark alley herself. For a moment she looked at the sea and sky. It wasn't the time to think of the dark. "What will you grow on your farm?"

He thought of it. At times like this he almost believed it would happen. "Corn, hay, some apples."

"And you have a house." Caught up, she twisted around to face him more directly. "A farmhouse?"

"It needs some work."

"It has a front porch? A big front porch?"

He laughed, pleasing her. "It's big enough. After I've replaced a few boards it might even be safe."

"On warm nights you'd sit out on a rocker and listen to the wind."

He tugged her hair. "The grass is always greener."

"So they say. Still, I think I could deal with fifty weeks of demands, of being on display, if only I had two weeks to sit on a rocker and listen to the wind. So you have land, a farmhouse, but no wife. Why?"

"An odd question from one's fiancée."

"You only say that to annoy me and evade answering."

"You're perceptive, Brie." He dropped off the wall and held out his hand. "We should be getting back."

"It only seems fair that I know more of your life when you know so much of mine." But she gave him her hand. "Have you ever been in love?"

"No."

"I wonder sometimes if I have." Her voice was wistful as she looked back out to sea. "That's why I goaded you into kissing me last night. I thought perhaps it might remind me."

He saw the humor in her statement, but he wasn't amused. "And did it?"

"No. It wasn't as though I'd never been kissed before, but it didn't bring anyone to mind."

Was she deliberately challenging him again, or was she just that artless? It didn't seem to matter. His hand slipped to her wrist. "No one?"

She heard the change, that gentle, dangerous tone. It was a tone a woman would be wise to be wary of. But she wasn't just a woman, Brie reminded herself as she lifted her head. She was a princess. "No one. It makes me think no man's been important to me before."

"You responded like a woman who knows what it is to want."

She didn't back away, though he was closer now. His face, she thought, wasn't one a woman would be comfortable with on long, rainy evenings. It would excite continually. His hands, large, elegant, strong, wouldn't make a woman dream softly. They'd make her pulse, even in sleep. She already knew it.

"Perhaps I am. After all, I'm not a child."

"No." He closed the gap. The wind whipped between them as he stepped forward. "Neither of us is."

Her mouth was soft, but it wasn't hesitant. It answered his, as it had the night before. No, life was never simple, he thought as he drew her closer. But God, it could be sweet.

She gave herself to him. Somehow she needed to just then with the sea thrashing below and the wind moaning. They were so alone it seemed right that they come together, body to body, mouth to mouth. She felt his hand slide up to her hair, firm, strong. As his fingers tangled in it, she let her head fall back. It wasn't surrender, but temptation.

His heartbeat was as hard and quick as hers. She could feel it pound against her. The sun was strong, so she kept her eyes closed until the light was red and warm. He tasted...enticing. Male, dark, not quite safe. She felt as if she were walking along the top of a wall, above the rock and water. It was frightening. Wonderful. She ran her hands up over his back. There was muscle there. Security. Danger. She wanted both. Just for a moment, this moment, she could be any woman. Even royalty bows to passion.

She was soft, but she wasn't safe. He knew it. He'd known it before he'd let himself be driven to touch her. Just as he knew he'd be driven to touch again and again what he beginning to crave. The scent she wore seemed to swim around him, lighter than the air, darker than the sea.

Did she know? Even as he submerged himself deeper in her, he wondered if she knew what she did. The eyes of a sorceress, the face of an angel. What man wouldn't be on his knees to her? Yet her sigh, quiet, low, was that of a woman. Flesh and blood or fairy tale, she was bound to tempt him. She wasn't meant to be resisted.

But he had no choice.

He drew her away much as he had the night before—slowly, reluctantly, but inevitably. Her eyes remained closed for just a moment longer, as if she were savoring the moment. But when they opened, her look was direct and level. Perhaps both of them knew they had to step back from the edge.

"Your family will wonder where you are."

She nodded, taking the final step back. "Yes. Obligations come first, don't they?"

He didn't answer, but they walked back to the car together.

Chapter 5

"Brie! Brie, wait a minute."

Turning, Brie shielded her eyes from the sun and watched Bennett step into the gardens with two Russian wolfhounds fretting at his heels.

His Royal Highness Prince Bennett de Cordina was dressed like a stablehand—worn jeans tucked into the tops of grimy boots, a shirt with a streak of dirt down one sleeve. As he drew closer, she caught the earthy smell of horses and hay on him. Like the dogs that fretted around his legs, he seemed to hold great stores of energy just under control.

"You're alone." He gave her a quick grin as he put one hand on the head of one dog and slipped another under

the collar of the second. "Easy, Boris," he said offhandedly as the dog tried to slobber over Brie's shoes.

Boris and...Natasha, she thought, flipping back in her
mental files for the names Reeve had given her. Even
dogs couldn't be ignored. They'd been a present to Bennett from the Russian ambassador, and with his penchant
for irony, Bennett had named them after characters in
an American cartoon show—inept Russian spies who
found it difficult to outwit a squirrel and a moose.

Bennett controlled his dogs—barely. "It's the first
morning I've seen you out."

"It's the first morning this week I haven't had meet-
ings." She smiled, not certain if she was guilty or
pleased. "Have you been riding?"

Did she ride? Her mind worked at the quick double
pace that was becoming familiar. She thought she knew
how to sit a horse, how to groom one. Brie struggled for
the sensation even while she smiled easily at her brother.

"Early. There was some work to do in the stables."
They stood awkwardly a moment as they both wondered what should be said. "You don't have your American shadow," Bennett blurted out, then grinned a little
sheepishly when Brie only lifted a brow. "Alex's nickname for Reeve," he said, and shrugged off any embarrassment. He generally found it a waste of time. "I like
him, actually. I think Alex does, too, or he'd be more

frigidly polite and pompous. It's just harder for him to accept an outsider right now."

"None of us were consulted about it, were we?"

"Well, he seems okay." Bennett let Boris rub up against him, not noticing or caring about the transfer of dog hair. "Not stuffy, anyway. I've been meaning to ask him where he gets his clothes."

She felt both tolerance and amusement, and wondered if this was habitual. "So the man might not be easily accepted, but his clothes are?"

"He certainly has an eye for them," Bennett commented as he pushed one of the dog's heads aside. "Does it bother you to have him around?"

Did it? Brie plucked a blossom from a creamy white azalea. It had been a week since she'd returned to the palace. A week since she'd returned to the life that wasn't yet her life. Feelings were something she had to reexplore every day.

She supposed she was nearly used to having Reeve there, at her side almost every waking moment. Yet she felt no less a stranger to him, to her family. To herself.

"No, but there are times when…" She looked out over the lush, blooming garden. Looked beyond. "Bennett, did I always have this need to get away? Everyone's so kind, so attentive, but I feel that if I could just go somewhere where I could breathe. Somewhere where I could lie on my back in the grass and leave everything behind."

"That's why you bought the little farm."

She turned back, brows knit. "Little farm?"

"We called it that, though it's really just a few acres of ground no one's ever done anything with. You threaten to build a house there from time to time."

A farmhouse, she mused. Perhaps that was why she'd felt so in tune with Reeve when they'd talked of his. "Is that where I was going when I…"

"Yes." The dogs were restless, so he let them go sniff around the bases of bushes and beat each other with their tails. "I wasn't here. I was at school. If father has his way, I'll be back at Oxford next week." Suddenly he looked as he was—a boy on the edge of manhood who had to bow to his father's wishes even as he strained against them. From somewhere inside Brie rose up an understanding and an affection. On impulse she linked her arm through his, and they began to walk.

"Bennett, do we like each other?"

"That's a silly—" He cut himself off and nudged at the dog that trotted alongside him. It wasn't as easy for him to control his emotions as it was for his father, for his brother. He had to concentrate on it, and as often as not, he still lost. But this was Brie; that made all the difference. "Yes, we like each other. It isn't easy to have friends, you know, who aren't somehow tied to our position. We're friends. You've always been my liaison to Father."

"Have I? In what way?"

"Whenever I'd get into trouble—"

"You have a habit of it?"

"Apparently." But he didn't sound displeased.

"And I don't?"

"You're more discreet." He gave her another of those quick, dashing smiles. "I've always admired the way you could do almost anything you wanted without making waves. I don't seem to be able to keep a low profile. I'm still dealing with the French singer fiasco."

"Oh?" Interested, she tilted her head up to look at him. God, she realized all at once. He was beautiful. There simply wasn't another word for it. If a woman drew an image of Prince Charming in her head, it would be Bennett. "A female singer, I take it."

"Lily." This time his smile didn't look young, but infinitely experienced. No, she realized, he wasn't really a boy, after all. "She was…talented," he decided with a flash of irony that was as mature as the smile. "And unsuitable. She sang in this little club in Paris. I spent a few weeks there last summer and we…we met."

"And had a blistering affair."

"It seemed like a good idea at the time. The press

licked their chops, rubbed their hands together and went to it. Lily's career skyrocketed." He smiled again, quick and crooked. "She got a recording contract and was— let's say she was very, very grateful."

"And you, of course, modestly accepted her gratitude."

"Of course. On the other hand, Father was furious. I'm sure he would have yanked me back to Cordina and put me in solitary confinement if you hadn't calmed him down."

She lifted both brows, impressed with herself. The man with the straight back and intense eyes wouldn't be easy to soothe. "Just how did I manage that?"

"If I knew how you get around him, Brie, I'd do my best to make it my own art."

She considered this, pleased and curious. "I must be good at it."

"The best. Father's fond of saying that of all his children, you're the only one with basic common sense."

"Oh, dear." She wrinkled her nose. "And you still like me?"

He did something so sweet, so natural, it brought tears to her eyes. He ruffled her hair. She blinked the tears away. "I'd just as soon you had the common sense. It would get in my way."

"And Alexander? How do I—you," she amended, "feel about him?"

"Oh, Alex is okay." He spoke with the tolerance of a brother for a brother. "He has the hardest road, after all, with the press forever hounding him and linking him with every woman he looks twice at. Discretion's an art with Alex. He has to be twice as good at everything, you know, because it's expected. And he has this roaring temper that he has to pull back. The heir isn't permitted to make public scenes. Even private ones can leak out. Remember when that overweight French count drank too much champagne at dinner and—" Smile fading, he broke off. "I'm sorry."

"No, don't be." She let out a sigh because the tension was back. "All this must be frustrating for you."

"For once I'm not thinking of myself." Then he stopped and took her hands. "Brie, when father called me at school and told me you'd been abducted—nothing's ever scared me like that. I hope nothing ever will again. It was as though someone drained the blood out of me—out of all of us. It's enough just to have you back."

She held his hands firmly. "I want to remember. When I do, we can walk in the gardens again and laugh over the French count who drank too much at dinner."

"Maybe you could let your memory be selective," he suggested. "I wouldn't mind you forgetting the time I put worms in your bed."

Brie's eyes widened as he continued to look at her. He was bland, innocent and attractive. "Neither would I."

"You didn't take it very well," he told her, thinking back. "Nanny gave me a tongue-lashing that left me raw for a week."

"Children have to be taught respect."

"Children?" This time he grinned and pinched her chin. "It was only last year." When she laughed he hesitated a moment, then gave in to the need and pressed his cheek against hers. "I miss you, Brie. Hurry back."

She rested there a moment, drawing in his scents, making him familiar. "I'll try."

He, more than anyone, understood that love had its own pressure. When he released her, his voice was light again, undemanding. "I've got to take the dogs back before they dig up the jasmine. Would you like me to walk you back?"

"No, I'll stay awhile. I have a fitting this afternoon for my dress for the AHC ball. I don't think I'll enjoy it."

"You detest it," Bennett said cheerfully. "I'll be done with Oxford and back for the ball." Done with Oxford, he thought again. The idea was nearly too good to be true. "I can dance with you while I look over the girls and decide which one I'm going to devastate."

She laughed. "I believe you have all the makings of a rake."

"I'm doing my best. Boris, Natasha." He called for the dogs and strolled out of the gardens with them scrambling at his heels.

She liked him. It relieved her to know it, to feel it. She might not remember the twenty years they'd shared together as brother and sister, but she liked the man he was today.

Sticking her hands in the pockets of her comfortable baggy slacks, Brie walked a little farther. The scents from the garden were mixed and heady, but not over-powering. The colors weren't a rainbow, but a kaleido-scope. As she walked, she tested herself. Without effort, she could identify each plant. The same way, she mused, she'd been able to identify the artists of the dozens of paintings in the Long Gallery in the west wing.

The artists, yes. But not the subjects. Her own mother's face would have been that of a stranger if Brie's resemblance to her hadn't been so strong. Looking at the portrait, Brie had seen where she'd inherited the color of her eyes, her hair, the shape of her face, her mouth. There was no doubt that Princess Elizabeth de Cordina had been more beautiful than her daughter. Brie could look at the painting and at the big, sweeping portrait of herself objectively and see this.

Princess Gabriella had been younger, twenty, twenty-one, Brie had decided. And she'd been rather spectacular in the deep violet dress she'd worn, its vivid pink sash a slash of heat. Looking at herself, Brie had wondered how she'd had the nerve to choose those shades for the sittings. And how she'd known they would be so effective.

But the face in her mother's portrait had been breathtaking. Heartbreaking. She'd worn creamy white, and had held soft pink roses that had given her a dreamy, poetic sort of beauty. Bennett had her look, as well as the spark of mischief Brie was certain she detected in the painting.

Alex was like their father—the military bearing, the intensity. She'd seen those qualities both in the flesh and in the official portraits. She wondered if Alex enjoyed the role of prince and heir or merely accepted it. More, she wondered if she and Alex had been close enough that she'd known his feelings, his hopes. She wondered when she'd know her own.

There was an arbor draped with wisteria and under it a pair of padded chairs and a marble table. Like the spot by the seawall, Brie felt a sense of comfort there.

It was easier to admit when she was alone that she still tired quickly. Sitting, Brie stretched out her legs, while the shade and muted light dappled over her. The blossoms had a sweet, undemanding scent. The drone of bees had a lazy sound. There didn't seem to be anything else. She closed her eyes and drifted.

* * *

Drowsy. She felt almost foolishly drowsy. It wasn't the comfortable, relaxed feeling she had come out to the country for. Whenever she drove out to the little farm it was to steal a little time away from Princess Gabriella for Brie Bisset. Time was precious. If she'd wanted a nap, she could have spent Sunday afternoon in her room.

Brie drank more of the coffee from her thermos. It was strong, the way she preferred it. The sun was warm, the bees humming. Yet she didn't seem to have the energy to walk as she'd planned. Perhaps she'd just close her eyes for a little while…. She couldn't seem to hold the coffee steadily in any case. Perhaps she'd just lean back against the rock and close her eyes….

Then the sun wasn't warm and strong any longer. There was a chill, as though the clouds had covered the sky and threatened rain. She couldn't smell the sweet grass, the sun-warmed flowers, but mustiness and damp. She hurt—ached all over, yet she hardly seemed to feel at all. Someone was talking, but she couldn't really hear. Mumbling, droning, but not bees. Men.

They'll make the exchange for the princess. They won't have a choice. Whispers, just whispers.

Tracks are covered. She'll sleep until morning. Deal with her again.

And she was afraid, terribly, paralyzingly afraid. She had to wake up. She had to wake up and—

"Brie."

With a muffled scream, she jolted in the chair, half springing up before hands closed over her arms. "No, don't! Don't touch me!"

"Easy." Reeve kept his hands firm as he lowered her back in her chair. She was cold, her eyes glazed. Thinking quickly, he decided that if she didn't calm within moments, he'd take her back to the palace and call Franco. "Just take it easy."

"I thought—" She glanced around quickly, the garden, the sun, the bees. When she discovered her heart was pounding, she made herself sit back and just breathe. "I must have been dreaming."

He studied her, searching for signs of shock. Apparently she wouldn't allow herself the luxury. "I wouldn't have woken you, but you looked like you were having a bad dream."

He released her only to sit in the chair beside her. He'd been there, beneath the wisteria, watching her sleep for five minutes, perhaps ten. She'd appeared so content, and he could look at her knowing the reserve she normally held herself in wasn't there.

He'd wanted to look at her, just look. There was no use

denying it to himself. When he watched her, he could remember her as she'd been years before, a young girl, pleased with herself, confident, innocently sensual. He could remember her as she'd been in his arms—a woman, arousing, bold, giving. He knew, as he looked at her, that he wanted her there again. And more.

Beyond that, he was aware that desire for her interfered with his objectivity. And a cop was nothing without objectivity, he knew. But he wasn't a cop any longer. Wasn't one of the reasons he'd turned in his badge that the constant struggle to be uninvolved and distant had become distasteful to him? He'd wanted something different in his life. He just hadn't counted on it being a princess.

He sat back, waiting until Brie's breathing steadied. For her sake, he'd better remember the rules he'd lived with during his years on the force. "Tell me," he said simply.

"There's not that much. It's confusing."

He took out a cigarette. "Tell me, anyway."

She sent him a look that he interpreted, correctly, as half resentment, half exasperation. It was better than neutrality. "I thought you were here as bodyguard, not analyst."

"I'm flexible." He lit the cigarette, watching her over the flame. "Are you?"

"Not very, I think." She rose. He'd already learned she rarely sat still when she was nervous. After she plucked off a spray of wisteria, she ran it lightly down her cheek. Another habit he'd noted. "I wasn't here, but someplace quiet. There was grass. I could smell it, very strong and sweet. It seemed I was sleepy, but I didn't want to be. It was annoying, because I was alone and wanted to enjoy the solitude."

This was accompanied by a look of pure defiance. Reeve merely nodded and leaned back. There was very little satisfaction in insulting him, Brie observed, and tucked the spray of wisteria in her hair.

"I was drinking coffee to try to stay awake."

His look sharpened, but she didn't notice. "Where did you get the coffee?"

"Where?" She frowned, finding it a foolish question when they were discussing a dream. "I had a thermos. A big, red thermos with the handle gone from the top. The coffee didn't seem to help and I dozed off. I remember the sun was very warm and I could hear the bees, just like now. Then…" He saw her fingers tense before she stuck them in her pockets. "I wasn't there any longer. It was dark and a bit damp. It smelled musty. There were voices."

He tensed, as well, but his voice was calm. "Whose?"

"I don't know. I didn't really hear them as much as

sense them. I was afraid." Turning away, she wrapped her arms around her body. "I was afraid and I couldn't wake up and stop the dream."

"Dream," he murmured. "Or memory?"

She whirled around, her eyes passionate again, her hands balled into fists inside her pockets. "I don't know. How can I? Do you think I can snap my fingers and say, ah, of course, I remember now?" She kicked at the little white stones along the edge of the path. "I walked with Bennett in the garden and all I could think was what a charming man. Damn! Is that the way I should think of my own brother?"

"He is a charming man, Gabriella."

"Don't patronize me," she said between her teeth. "Don't you dare patronize me."

He smiled at that, because whether she knew it or not at that moment, she was all princess. Royalty flowed through her—somehow admirable and amusing to a man who'd seen his share of aristocrats. Still, he rose and spoke gently. "Who thinks you should snap your fingers, Brie? No one's pressuring you but yourself."

"I'm pressured by kindness."

"Don't worry," he said with a shrug. "I won't be kind to you."

"I can depend on it." She paused a moment, frowning at him. "You said once before that I was selfish. Why?"

Without thinking, he ran a finger between her brow where the line of temper formed. "Perhaps the word should be 'self-absorbed.' You may have a right to be at the moment."

"I'm not sure I like that any better. You also said spoiled."

"Yes." He let his hand fall away so that they faced each other without touching.

"I refuse to accept that."

"Sorry."

Her eyes narrowed. "You're sorry because you said it?"

"No, because you refuse to accept what you are."

"You're a rude man, Reeve MacGee. Rude and opinionated."

"True enough," he agreed, and rocked back on his heels. "I also said you were willful."

Her chin came up. "That I accept," she told him coolly. "But you haven't the right to say it to me."

He gave her a very slow, very arrogant bow. It wasn't difficult when she chose to play the princess for him to play the pauper. "I beg your pardon, Your Highness."

Fire flared, in her blood, in her eyes. She found the fingers in her pockets itched to make solid contact with his face. Breeding hampered her, and she found she didn't care for the restriction. "Now you're mocking me."

Nora Roberts

"We'll add 'astute' to the list."

Amazed at how quickly the anger rose, she took another step toward him. "You seem to be going out of your way to insult me. Why?"

There was something irresistible about her when she was haughty, angry, icy. Reeve took her face in one hand, holding it firmly when her mouth dropped open in surprise. "Because it makes you think of me. I don't give a damn how you think of me, Gabriella, as long as you do."

"Then you have your wish," she said evenly. "I do think of you, but I don't think well of you."

He smiled slowly. She found this made her throat dry and her skin hot. "Just think of me," he repeated. "I won't strew roses on the floor when I lead you to bed. There won't be any violins, and satin sheets. What there'll be is you and me."

She didn't step back. Whether it was shock or excitement that kept her still she didn't know. Perhaps it was pride. That's what she hoped. "You seem to be the one in need of the analyst now. I may not remember, Reeve, but I feel certain I choose my own lovers."

"So do I."

She felt light-headed. Frightened? No—yes. When he spoke she felt the decision had already been made. Another lack of choice. "Take your hands off me." She said it quietly, with a hint of arrogance that hid the fear.

He drew her closer, just a little closer. "Is that a royal command?"

She might have been wearing a robe and a crown. "Take it however you choose. You need my permission to touch me, Reeve. A man of your background knows the rules."

"Americans aren't as subject to protocol as Europeans, Brie." His lips hovered over hers, but didn't quite touch. "I want to touch you, so I touch. I want you, so I'll take—when the time's right for both of us." As he said this, his fingers tightened.

Her vision blurred, her knees shook. It was dark again, and the face close to hers was indistinct. She smelled wine, strong and stale. Fear tripled, pulsing through her like a drug. Abruptly she struck out at him, swaying as she did. "Don't touch me! Don't! *Relâchez-moi, salaud—*"

Because her voice was more desperate than angry, he let her go, then almost immediately grabbed her again when she swayed forward. "Brie." He had her back in the chair, her head between her knees, before she could think. Silently cursing himself, his voice was gentle, calming. "Breathe deep and relax. I'm sorry. I've no intention of taking any more than you want to give."

He wouldn't. No, he wouldn't. Her eyes shut, she tried to clear her mind, clear the dizziness.

"No." When she struggled against his hand, he released her. Her face was still pale when she looked up at him, but her eyes were dark and intense. Terrified. "It wasn't you," she managed. "It wasn't you at all. I remembered—I think…" On a frustrated breath, she closed her eyes again and fought for composure. "It was someone else. Just for a minute I was somewhere else. A man was holding me. I can't see him—it's dark or my mind just won't let me get through to his face. But he's holding me and I know, I know he'll rape me. He's drunk."

Her hand reached out for Reeve's and held it. "I could smell the wine on him. Just now I could smell it. His hands are rough. He's very strong, but he's had too much wine." She swallowed. Reeve saw her shudder just before she took her hand from him and straightened in her chair. "I had a knife. I don't know how. I had a knife and its handle was in my hand. I think I killed him."

She looked down at her hand. It was steady. Turning it over, she stared down at her palm. It was white and smooth. "I think I stabbed him with the knife," she said calmly. "And his blood was on my hands."

"Brie." Reeve started to reach out for her, then thought better of it. "Tell me what else you remember."

She looked at him then and her face was as it had been in the hospital. Colorless and strained. "Nothing. I only remember struggling and the smells. I can't be sure if I killed him. There's nothing after the struggle, nothing before." She folded her hands in her lap and looked beyond him. "If the man raped me, I don't remember it."

He wanted to swear again, and barely controlled the impulse. Everything she said made his little power play of a few moments before seem hard and crude. "You weren't sexually assaulted," he told her in brisk, practical tones. "The doctors were very thorough."

Relief threatened to come in tears. She held them back. "But they can't tell me if I killed a man or not."

"No. Only you can   when you're ready."

She merely nodded, then forced herself to look at him again. "You've killed before."

He took another cigarette and lit it with a barely restrained violence. "Yeah."

"You—in your work. It was necessary for defense, protection?"

"That's right."

"When it's necessary, it doesn't leave any scars, does it?"

He could lie, make it easy for her. He was tempted to. When he looked at her, her eyes were so troubled. Inadvertently he'd forced a memory out of her. A dark, horrible memory. Did that make him responsible? Hadn't he already chosen to be responsible?

He could lie, but when she learned the truth, it would

be that much worse. Yes, he'd chosen to be responsible. "It leaves scars," he said briefly, and rose, taking her hand as he did. "You can live with scars, Brie."

She'd known it. Even before she'd asked, before he'd answered, she'd known it. "Do you have many?"

"Enough. I decided I couldn't live with any more."

"So you bought a farm."

"Yeah." He tossed down the cigarette. "I bought a farm. Maybe next year I'll even plant something."

"I'd like to see it." She saw his quick, half-amused look, and felt foolish. "Sometime, perhaps."

He wanted her to, and felt foolish. "Sure, sometime."

Brie let her hand stay in his as they walked through the gardens, back toward the white, white walls of the palace.

Chapter 6

Barefoot, wrapped only in a thin silk robe, Brie sat dutifully on the bed while Dr. Franco took her blood pressure. His hands were deft, his manner kind, almost fatherly. Still, she wasn't entirely accepting of the weekly examinations by her family's doctor. Nor was she resigned to the biweekly sessions with his associate, Dr. Kijinsky, the eminent and scholarly psychiatrist. She wasn't an invalid, and she wasn't ill.

True, she tired more easily than she might have liked, but her strength was coming back. And her sessions with the renowned analyst, Dr. Kijinsky, were no more than conversations. Conversations, she mused, that were really no more than a waste of time. And it was time, after all, that she was so determined to recover.

The plans for the charity ball the first week of June were her priority. Food, wine, music, decorations. Entertainment, acceptances, regrets, requests. Even though she seemed to enjoy the preparations, they weren't easy. When someone paid a good sum of money to attend an affair, charitable or not, he expected and deserved the best. She'd spent three long, testy hours with the florist just that morning to guarantee the finest.

"Your pressure is good." Franco tucked the gauge back into his bag. "And your pulse, your color. Physically, there seem to be no complications. My complaint would be that you're still a bit thin. Five pounds wouldn't hurt you."

"Five pounds would throw my dressmaker into a frenzy," she returned with a half smile. "She's thrilled with me at the moment."

"Bah." Franco rubbed a hand over his trim white beard. "She looks for a coat hanger to drape her material on. You need some flesh, Gabriella. Your family has always tended to be just a bit too slim. Are you taking the vitamins I prescribed?"

"Every morning."

"Good. Good." He pulled off his stethoscope, dropping that into the bag, as well. "Your father tells me you haven't cut back on your schedule."

Her defenses came up immediately. "I like being busy."

"That hasn't changed. My dear..." Setting his bag aside, he sat down on the bed next to her. The informality surprised her only because she'd become accustomed to the rules she was bound by. Yet Franco seemed so at ease she decided they must have sat just this casually dozens of times. "As I said, physically, you're recovering perfectly. I have great respect for Dr. Kijinsky's talents, or I wouldn't have recommended him. Still, I'd like you to tell me how you feel."

Brie folded her hands in her lap. "Dr. Franco—"

"You're weary of doctors," he said with a wave of his hand. "You're annoyed by the prodding, the poking, the sessions. Questions, you think, too many questions. You want to get on with your life."

She smiled, more amused than disconcerted. "It doesn't seem you need me to tell you how I feel. Do you always read your patient's mind, Dr. Franco?"

He didn't smile, but his eyes remained kind, tolerant. All at once, she felt petty and rude. "I'm sorry." She touched him because it was her nature to do so when she apologized, and meant it. "That sounded sarcastic. I didn't mean it to be. The truth is, Dr. Franco, I feel so many things—too many things. Everyone I know seems to understand them before I do."

"Do you feel we're simplifying your amnesia?"

"No…" Unsure, she shook her head. "It just seems as though it's taken for granted that it's a small problem that should resolve itself. Politically, I suppose it's necessary to think that."

The resentment, ever so slightly, was there. Franco, who knew what her father was going through, refrained from commenting directly. "No one, especially your doctor, makes light of what you're going through. Yet it's difficult for those around you, those close to you, to fully understand and accept. It's because of this that I'd like you to talk to me."

"I'm not sure what I should say—even what I want to say."

"Gabriella, I brought you into the world. I ministered to your sniffles, treated you through chicken pox and took out your tonsils. Your body is no stranger to me, nor is your mind." He paused while she took this in. "You have difficulty talking to your father for fear of hurting him."

"Yes." She looked at him then, the pleasant face, the white beard. "Him most of all. Before Bennett left—he went grumbling back to Oxford yesterday."

"He'd prefer to stay here with his dogs and horses."

"Yes." She laughed, shaking back her hair. "With Bennett here, it was easier somehow. He's so relaxed and open. With him I didn't always feel compelled to say the right things—the kind thing. Alexander's different. I feel I should be very careful around him. He's so, well, proper."

"'Prince Perfect.'" Franco smiled at her expression. The vague disapproval was a good sign. "No disrespect, Gabriella. You and Bennett dubbed him so when you were children."

She nearly smiled herself. "How nasty."

"Oh, he can handle himself. Bennett's called 'Lord Sloth.'"

She made a sound suspiciously like a giggle and folded her legs under her. "Natural enough. I volunteered to help him pack. It wasn't easy to believe anyone could live in such a sty. And me?" She lifted a brow. "Did my brothers give me a title?"

"'Her Obstinacy.'"

"Oh." Brie sat for a moment, then chuckled. "I take it I deserved it."

"Then and now, it suits."

"I think—I feel," Brie amended, "that we're a close family. Is this true?"

A simple yes would mean nothing, Franco thought. A simple yes was too easy. "Once a year you go to Zurich, *en famille*. For two weeks there are no servants, no outsiders. You told me once that this was what helped you cope with the other fifty weeks."

She nodded, accepting. And, gratefully, understanding. "Tell me how my mother died, Dr. Franco."

"She was delicate," he said carefully. "She was speaking for the Red Cross in Paris and contracted pneumonia. There were complications. She never recovered."

She wanted to feel. It would be a blessing to feel grief, pain, but there was nothing. Folding her hands again, she looked down at them. "Did I love her?"

Compassion wasn't something a doctor carried in his bag, but something he carried with him. "She was the center of your family. The anchor, the heart. You loved her, Gabriella, very much."

Believing it was almost, almost as comforting as feeling it. "How long was she ill?"

"Six months."

The family would have drawn together, knotted together. Of that she was certain. "We don't accept outsiders easily."

Franco smiled again. "No."

"Reeve MacGee, you know him?"

"The American?" Franco moved his shoulders in a gesture Brie recognized as French and pragmatic. "Only slightly. Your father thinks highly of him."

"Alexander resents him."

"Naturally enough." Franco spoke slowly, intrigued by the turn of the conversation. Perhaps she didn't know her family yet, but they were still, as they had always been, her chief concern. "Prince Alexander feels protective of you, and doesn't welcome the assistance of anyone outside the family. The pretense of your engagement..." He paused at Brie's narrowed look, but misinterpreted it. "I don't gossip. As physician to the royal family, I'm in your father's confidence."

She unfolded her legs and rose, no longer content to sit. "And do you agree with his opinion?"

Franco lifted one bushy white brow. "I wouldn't presume to agree or disagree with Prince Armand, except on medical matters. However, the engagement is bound to annoy your brother, who feels personally responsible for your welfare."

"And my feelings?" Abruptly her calm vanished. She turned to where the doctor now stood beside her bed, his hands locked comfortably behind his back. "Are they considered? This—this pretense that all is well, this farce that I've had a whirlwind romance with the son of my father's friend. They infuriate me."

She snatched up a mother-of-pearl comb from her dresser and began to tap it against her palm. "The announcement of my engagement was made only yesterday, and already the papers are full of it. Crammed with their speculation, their opinions, their chatty little stories. Everywhere I go there are questions and flutters and sighs."

The impatience was obvious and, to the doctor, familiar. With his fingers still linked behind his back, he remained silent and waited for it to run its course.

"Just this morning while I'm trying to organize for the ball, I'm asked about my wedding dress. Will it be white or ivory? Will I use my dressmaker, or go to Paris as my mother did? My wedding dress," she repeated tossing up her hands. "When I have to finalize a menu for fifteen hundred people. Will I have the ceremony in the palace chapel or the cathedral? Will my good friends from college be in the wedding party? Will I choose the English princess or the French countess as my maid of honor—neither of whom I remember in the slightest. The more we try to gloss over and hide what's real, what's true, the more absurd it becomes."

"Your father is protecting your welfare, Gabriella, and his people's."

"Are they never two separate things?" she demanded, then tossed the comb back on the dresser. "I'm sorry." Her voice calmed. "That was unfair. Deception is difficult. It seems I'm involved in it on so many levels. And Reeve—" Brie broke off, annoyed with herself for permitting her thoughts to travel in his direction.

"Is attractive," Franco finished.

With a slow cautious smile, she studied her doctor. "You're an excellent physician, Dr. Franco."

He gave her a quick, dapper bow. "I know my patients, Your Highness."

"Attractive," she agreed. "But not in all ways likable. I don't find his consistent dominance particularly appealing, especially in the role of fiancé. However, I'll play my part. When my memory returns, the American can go back to his farm, I can go back to my life. That's how I feel, Dr. Franco." She put both hands on the back of a chair. "That, simply stated, is how I feel. I want to remember. I want to understand. And I want to get back to my life."

"You'll remember, Gabriella."

"You can be sure?"

"As a doctor, nothing is ever sure." Bending, wheezing a bit with the movement, he picked up his bag again. "As someone who's known you from the cradle, I'm sure."

"That's the opinion I prefer." She stepped forward toward the door.

"No need to see me out." He brushed her back with the habitual pat on the hand. "I'll give your father my assurances before I go."

"Thank you, Dr. Franco."

"Gabriella." He paused with the door just opened. "We all have our pretenses to keep up."

The inclination of her head was cool and regal. "So I understand."

Discreetly she waited until the door closed behind him before she whirled away, fuming. Pretenses. Yes, she'd play them, she'd accept them. But she detested them. With her temper unsteady, she pulled out of the trash the paper she'd wadded up and discarded that morning.

PRINCESS GABRIELLA TO WED

Brie swore as princesses are only allowed to do in private. There was a picture of her and one of Reeve. With her head tilted and the sun streaming in on the newsprint, she studied him.

Attractive, yes, she decided. In that just-on-the-edge-of-rough, just-on-the-edge-of-sleek sort of way. Like a big predatory cat, she mused, who could swagger away or pounce as the mood struck. He'd make his own choices. A man like that caused mixed feelings. Not only in her, she noted with some satisfaction. The press was of two minds, as well.

There was obvious excitement and a proprietary sort of satisfaction that one of the royal children was to wed. It was pointed out, she noted, that she, of all the princesses in the history of Cordina, had waited the longest to take the plunge. About time, the paper seemed to say with a brisk nod.

The family tie between the Bissets and MacGees counted in Reeve's favor, as did his father's reputation. But he was, after all, an American, and not precisely the ideal choice according to the citizens of Cordina.

Whatever satisfaction Brie might have gained from that was offset by the mention of several more eligible options. It was disconcerting to find herself matched, if only in the press, with a half a dozen eligible bachelors. Princes, lords, marquesses, tycoons. Obviously from the brief stories attached to the pictures, she'd met and spent time with them all. One of them might have meant something to her, but she had no way of being sure. She could study their names and faces for five minutes, an hour, but there'd be no change. She turned back to Reeve. At least with him, she knew where she stood.

Apparently the press was prepared to reserve final judgment on the American ex-policeman—son of a well-known and respected diplomat. Instead it chose to speculate on the wedding date.

She tossed the paper on the bed so that it fell with the photos up. Her father had accomplished his purpose, she reflected. The focus was on the engagement rather than the kidnapping. No one would question Reeve's presence in the palace, or his place at her side.

No one would question him—no one would question her. Slowly Brie turned her hands over and stared down at them. There was something she'd been unable to speak of to either of her doctors. Something she'd been unable to put into words to anyone other than Reeve.

Had she killed a man? Had she taken a knife and... Good God, when would she know?

Trying to force herself to remember brought nothing but frustration. Concentration on this would cause her head to pound until she couldn't concentrate on anything at all. What snatches came, came in dreams. And like dreams, when she awoke the images were vague and distorted. But the images, rather than easing the pressure, only increased it. Every morning she lay quietly, hoping the memories would come naturally. Every day there was only the dregs of dreams.

She could work, Brie reminded herself. Filling the hours each day was anything but a problem. The work was enjoyable, fulfilling—but for the fact that she now had this foolish engagement to contend with. The sooner she could brush that aside and go on, the better. She'd view it as one more goal to reach—or one more obstacle to overcome.

"Come in." She answered the knock at the door, but

she was frowning. The frown didn't diminish when Reeve walked in.

"Surely I'm considered safe in my own bedroom."

The room smelled subtly of flowers. They were there in a vase on a table by the window, on a stand beside the bed. Through the open window, the breeze traveled in and tossed the scent everywhere. "Dr. Franco says you're recovering nicely."

Brie deliberately took her time settling on the long, cushioned window seat. It gave her the opportunity to control her temper. "Does the doctor report to you, as well?"

"I was with your father." He saw the newspaper on the bed, the photos, but said nothing. It wouldn't do to admit that the front-page splash had given him quite a jolt that morning. It was one thing to agree to a mock engagement, and another to see evidence of it in black and white.

Instead he wandered over to her dresser and idly picked up a small glass jar. He'd concentrate on that for a moment until he could forget just the way she looked in that thin ivory robe. "So you're feeling better?"

"I'm quite well, thank you."

The icily formal reply had his lips twitching. She wouldn't give an inch, Reeve mused. So much the better.

"How's your schedule for tomorrow?" he asked, though he'd already made it his business to know.

"I'm not free until after noon. Then there's nothing until dinner with the Duke and Duchess of Marlborough and Monsieur Loubet and his wife."

If Reeve read her tone correctly, she wasn't looking forward to the dinner any more than he was. It would be their first as an officially engaged couple. "Then perhaps you'd like to go sailing for a few hours in the afternoon."

"Sailing?" He watched her eyes light up just before she swept her lashes down and spoke coolly. "Is this an invitation or a way to keep me supervised?"

"Both." He opened the jar, dipped a finger into the cream and rubbed it between his thumb and forefinger. It smelled like her skin—soft and sexy. At night, he imagined, and in the mornings, she'd smooth on the cream until its fragrance was part of her.

He was here to protect her, he thought ruefully as he closed the jar again, but who was going to protect him? As she sat in silence, he put down the jar and crossed to her.

"If you want to weigh the pros and cons, Brie, consider that you'll be away from the palace and responsibility for a few hours."

"With you."

"Engaged couples are expected to spend some time

together," he said easily, then put a firm hand on her arm before she could jump up. "You agreed," he said with the steel just below the calm tone. "Now you have to follow through."

"Only in public."

"A woman in your position has little private life. And," he continued, moving his hand down to hers, "I've put mine under the microscope, as well."

"You want gratitude? I find it difficult right at the moment."

"Keep it." Annoyed, he tightened his grip until her eyes met his. "Cooperation's enough."

Her chin was up, her eyes level. "Yours or mine?"

He inclined his head slightly. "The answer seems to be both again. Officially, we're engaged. In love," he added, testing the words.

The words worried her. "Officially," she agreed. "It's simply a trapping."

"Trappings can be convenient. And since we're on the subject..." Reaching into his pocket, Reeve brought out a small velvet box. With his thumb he flipped up the top. The sun shot down and seemed to explode within the white, square-cut diamond.

Brie felt her heart begin to thud in her breast, then her throat. "No."

"Too traditional?" Reeve drew the ring out of the box

and twisted it in the sunlight. The white stone was suddenly alive with color. "It suits you. Clean, cool, elegant. Ready to give off passion at the right touch." He was no longer looking at the diamond, but at her. "Give me your hand, Gabriella."

She didn't move. Perhaps foolishly, she felt she didn't have to. "I won't wear your ring."

He took her left wrist and felt the pulse thud under his fingers. The sun poured through the window, showering on her hair, into her eyes. The fury was there—he could feel it. And the passion. Hardly romantic, he thought as he pushed the ring onto her finger. But, then, romance wasn't the order of the day.

"Yes, you will." He closed his hand over hers, sealing the bond. He didn't allow himself to think just yet of how difficult it might be to break.

"I'll just take it off again," she told him furiously.

He spoke in a tone she didn't trust. "That wouldn't be wise."

"Still following my father's orders?" she said between her teeth.

"It seems we both are. But the ring was my idea." He cupped the back of her neck with his free hand. It was long and slender and smooth. "So's this."

When he kissed her, he gave her no choice. She stiff-ened; he stroked. She shuddered; he soothed. The moment he felt her respond, he took her deep and fast.

His fingers were in her hair, his hand on hers, yet her body throbbed as though he touched everywhere. She would have welcomed that. The mouth didn't seem to be enough to give, to take, to demand. Whole worlds opened up and spun at the touch of mouth to mouth. She could taste what he offered—passion, wild, ripe, frec. Fulfillment was there, churning within her if she chose to let go.

She came alive when he held her. Reeve hadn't known a woman could be so electric while remaining so soft. He could feel pulse beats, tempting him to touch them, one by one. He started with her throat, just a skim of a fingertip. Her moan rippled into his mouth. The inside of her elbow—the blood pounded there. At her wrist it jumped frantically.

He drew her bottom lip into his mouth to suck, to nibble. Her body trembled, arousing him beyond belief as he took his hand slowly up from her waist to find her breast. The thin robe she wore could have been pulled away with one hand, leaving her naked, but Reeve kept the barrier knowing his sanity would be pulled away with it.

When he made love with her, fully, completely, there wouldn't be servants or staff or family. When he made love with her the first time, there'd be nothing, no one but the two of them. She'd never forget it. Or him.

He ran his hand down her once, one long, firm stroke. Possession, threat, promise. Neither of them could be sure which. When he let her go, neither of them was steady.

Brie saw something in his eyes that had her skin heating. Desire, but more. Knowledge. His eyes were blue, dark, not quite calm. In them she saw the knowledge that she wouldn't walk away from him easily. Not today. Not tomorrow.

She drew back against the window seat, as far away from him as she could. "You have no right."

He looked at her until she had to hold back the tremble. "I don't need any." When he reached up to cup her face she went still. It was a habit of his she hadn't quite fathomed. It might be gentleness; it might be arrogance. "I don't want any."

Her strength was nothing to be underestimated. She was still, yes, but she wasn't weak. "I'll tell you when I want to be touched, Reeve."

He didn't remove his hand. "So you have."

Try a different tactic, she decided. Something had to work. "I think you're taking this charade too seriously. You overstep yourself."

"If you want bows and protocol, you'll have to look elsewhere. Remember, you told me not to be kind."

"A request that isn't difficult for you."

"Not at all." He smiled, then lifted her hand where the diamond flashed. "You and I know this is no more than a pretty rock, Brie. Another trapping." On impulse, he turned her hand over, held it, then pressed his lips to her palm. "No one else will."

This time she jerked her hand away and rose. "I told you I won't wear it."

Before she could pull the ring off he was beside her. "And I told you you would. Think." When she paused, the ring half off her finger, he continued. The tone he used was precisely the tone he used to draw the answer he wanted out of reluctant suspects. Deals, he thought ruefully, were deals. "Would you rather swallow your pride and wear it, or explain every time you go out why you don't have an engagement ring?"

"I could say I don't care for jewelry."

He grinned, touching the sapphires on her right hand, then the deep-blue stones she wore at her ears. "Could you? Some lies are more easily believed than others."

Brie pushed the ring back on. "Damn you."

"Better," he said with a nod of approval. "Curse me as much as you like, just cooperate. It might occur to you, Your Highness, that I'm just as inconvenienced by all this as you."

Trapped, she turned away. "Inconvenienced? You seem to be enjoying it."

"I'm making the best of a bargain. You could do the same, or you can stomp your feet."

She whirled back around, eyes flashing. "I don't make a habit of temper tantrums."

"Could have fooled me."

She calmed, only because to have let loose would have gratified him. "I don't like it when you make me feel like a child, Reeve."

His voice was equally calm. "Then don't object when I make you feel like a woman."

"Have you an answer for everything?"

He thought of her, of what was growing inside him. Briefly he touched her cheek. "No. A truce for the moment, Brie. Before this business of the engagement came up we got along well enough. Look at it as a simplification."

She frowned, but discovered she was willing to call a truce. Until she had her full strength back. "A simplification of what?"

"Of everything. With this—" he lifted her left hand again "—you won't have to explain why we spend time together, what I'm doing here. As an engaged couple we can get out a bit, get away. People are tolerant of lovers escaping. You won't be as tied to the palace."

"I never said I felt tied."

"I've seen you looking out the window. Any window."

Her gaze came back to him and held. Abruptly she surrendered and, with a sigh, sat back on the window seat. "All right, yes, sometimes I feel closed in. None of this is familiar to me, and yet it isn't altogether strange. It isn't a comfortable feeling, Reeve, to feel as though you belong, but never being quite sure you won't make a wrong turn and find yourself lost again. And the dreams—" She broke off, cursing herself. It was too easy to say more to him than was comfortable.

"You've had more dreams?"

"Nothing I remember very well."

"Brie." The patience wasn't there as it had been with Franco, but the knowledge was.

"It's true, I don't." Frustrated, she pulled her fingers through her hair. He saw his ring throw out fire against the fire. His fire, he thought. And hers. "It's always basically the same—the dark, the smells, the fear. I don't have anything tangible, Reeve." For a moment she closed her eyes tight. Weakness was so easy. Tears were so simple. She wouldn't allow them for herself. "There's nothing for me to hold on to. Every morning I tell myself this could be the day the curtain lifts. And every night…" She shrugged.

He wanted to go to her, hold her. Passion he could offer safely. Comfort was dangerous. He kept his distance. "Tomorrow you won't have to think about it. We'll go out on the water. Just sail. Sun and sea, that's all. There won't be anyone there you have to play a role for."

A few hours without pretenses, she thought. He was offering her a gift. Perhaps he was taking one for himself, but he was entitled. Brie looked down at her ring, then up at him. "Nor you."

He smiled. She thought it was almost friendly. "Agreed."

Chapter 7

Like too many other things, Brie had forgotten what it was to really relax. Learning how was a discovery in pleasure, and one that was blissfully easy. She hoped that when other memories came back to her, they'd be as sweet.

Still, she'd found one more thing she could be certain of. She was as at home on the sea as she was on land. It was a simple pleasure—as relaxing was—and therefore an important one, to find that she knew her way around canvas and rope. If she'd been alone on the pretty little sloop, Brie could have sailed her. She'd have had the control, the knowledge and the strength. Of that she was certain.

She could listen to the noise of the water against the

hull as the boat gathered speed and know she'd heard the sound before. It didn't matter where or how.

She loved to sail. Everyone Reeve had spoken to had confirmed it. The idea for a day on the water had come to him when he'd noticed that the finely strung nerves, the strain and the depression hadn't eased. Not as much as she pretended. She'd told him not to be kind, but it wasn't always possible to follow even the orders of a princess.

Relying on his instincts, he'd let her take the tiller when they'd cast off. Now he watched her turn it slightly, away from the wind. In accord, he pulled in on the main-sheet to quiet and stretch the flapping canvas. As the boat sped across the wind, it gathered more speed. He heard Brie laugh as the sails filled.

"It's wonderful," she called. "The best. So free, so simple."

The wind exhilarated her. Speed, on this first run, seemed to be imperative. Power, after being for so long under the power of others, was intoxicating. Control—at last she'd found something she could control. Her hand was light on the tiller, adjusting, as Reeve did, whenever it was necessary to keep the pace at maximum.

Walls, obligations, responsibilities disappeared. All that was left was water and wind. Time wasn't impor-tant here. She could push it aside, as perhaps she'd done before. As she now knew she'd do again. The sun was as it should be on a holiday. Bright, full, warm—gold in the sky, white on the sea. Holding the tiller steady with her knee, Brie slipped out of the oversized cotton shirt. Her brief bikini made a shrug at modesty. She wanted the sun on her skin, the wind on it. Skillfully she navigated so that she avoided any other boats. Privacy she wouldn't sacrifice.

For a few hours she'd be selfish. For a few hours she didn't have to be a princess, but only a woman, stroked by the wind, soothed by the sun. With another laugh she shook back her hair, only to have the wind swirl through it again.

"I've done this before."

Reeve relaxed; the wind was doing the work for the moment. "It's your boat," he said easily. "According to your father, Bennett can outride anyone, Alexander can outfence the masters, but you're the best sailor in the family."

Thoughtful, Brie ran a hand along the glossy mahogany rail. "*Liberté,*" she mused, thinking of the name on the stern. "It would seem that like the little farm, I use this for an escape."

Reeve turned to look at her. Through his amber-tinted glasses she looked gold and lush. Primitive, desirable, but still somehow lost. Whatever his inclinations, it wouldn't do to be too kind. "I'd say you were entitled. Wouldn't you?"

She made a little sound, noncommittal, unsure. "It only makes me wonder if I was happy before. I find myself thinking sometimes that when I remember, I'll wish I'd let things stand as they are now. Everything's new, you understand?"

"A fresh start?" He thought of his own farm, his own fresh start. But, then, he'd known where he'd ended, where he'd begun.

"I'm not saying I don't want to remember." She watched Reeve pull his T-shirt over his head and discard it. He looked so natural, she thought, so at ease with himself. His trunks were brief, but she felt no self-consciousness. She'd been held against that body. Brie let herself remember it. He was lean, hard. Little drops of spray glistened on his skin. A dangerous man. But wasn't danger something she'd have to face sooner or later?

Yes, she remembered his embrace. Should she be ashamed to discover she wanted to be held against him, by him, again? She wasn't ashamed, she realized, whether she should be or not. But she was cautious. "I know so little," she murmured. "Of myself. Of you."

Reeve took a cigarette from the shirt he'd tossed on the bench. He cupped his hands, flicked his lighter, the movements economical. As he blew out smoke, he looked at her again. "What do you want to know?"

She didn't answer for a moment, but studied him. This was a man who could take care of himself, and others when he chose. This was a man, she was all but certain, who made his own rules. And yet...unless she was very mistaken, he was a man who'd lived by rules already set for most of his life. Which was he doing now? "My father trusts you."

Reeve nodded, making the adjustments as the sail began luffing. "He has no reason not to."

"Still, it's your father he knows well, not you."

His lips curved. The arrogance was there again, she thought, no matter how elegant, how well groomed he was. It was, unfortunately, one of the most attractive things about him.

"Don't you trust me, Gabriella?" He made his voice deliberately low, deliberately challenging. He was baiting her; they both knew it. So her answer, when she gave it, left him speechless.

"With my life," she said simply. She turned into the wind again and let the boat race.

What could he say to her? There'd been no guile in her words, no irony. She meant exactly what she'd said, not merely the phrase but the intent. He should have been pleased. Her trust, theoretically, would simplify his job.

So why did he feel uncomfortable with it, wary of it? Of it, he asked himself, or of her?

It came back to him now what he'd realized from the first moment he'd seen her again in the hospital bed. Nothing between them would ever be casual. In the same way, he was all but sure nothing between them could ever be serious. So he was caught, very much as Brie was, in an odd sort of limbo.

They were both, in their own ways, beginning a new life. Neither of them had any reason to want the other complicating it. The truth was that Reeve had made himself a promise to simplify his life. Almost as soon as he'd begun, there had been the call from Cordina, and things had become tangled again.

He could have said no, Reeve reminded himself. He hadn't wanted to. Why? Because Brie, as she'd been at sixteen, had stayed in his mind for too many years.

Since he'd come to Cordina, things had only become more involved. The bogus engagement had the international press kicking up their heels. A royal wedding was always good copy. Already three of the top American magazines were begging for interviews. The paparazzi were there like eager little terriers every time he or Brie stepped out of the palace.

He could have refused Prince Armand's request that he pretend to be engaged to Brie. The fact that it was a logical solution to a delicate problem was outweighed by the nuisance value. But he hadn't wanted to. Why? Because Brie, the woman he was coming to know, was threatening to stay in his mind for a lifetime.

Being with her, and not being with her, was like taking a long, slow walk a few inches over very hot coals. The steam was there, the sizzle—but it wasn't possible to cool off or take the fatal plunge into the heat.

"That little cove." Brie lifted her hand to point. "It looks quiet."

Without fuss, they began to tack toward the small shelter. She worked with the wind, coaxing it, bowing to it. Once the lines were secure, Bric merely sat, staring across the narrow strip of water.

"From here Cordina looks so fanciful. So pink and white and lovely. It seems as though nothing bad would ever happen there."

He looked with her. "Fairy tales are traditionally violent, aren't they?"

"Yes." She smiled a little, looking up at the palace. How bold it looked, she thought. How bold and elegant. "But, then, no matter how much it looks like one, Cordina isn't a fairy tale. Does your practical, democratic American mind find it foolish—our castles, our pomp and protocol?"

This time he smiled. Perhaps she didn't remember

her roots, but they were there, dug in. "I find it intelligently run. Lebarre is one of the best ports in the world, regardless of size. Culturally, Cordina bows to no one. Economically, it's sound."

"True. I, too, have been doing my homework. Still..." Brie ran her tongue over her teeth before she leaned back and circled her knee with her arms. "Did you know that women weren't granted the right to vote in Cordina until after World War II? Granted, as though it were a favor, not a right. Family life is still very Mediterranean, with the wife subservient and the husband dominant."

"In theory, or in practice?" Reeve countered.

"From what I've seen, very much in practice. Constitutionally, the title my father holds can pass only to a male."

Reeve listened, looking across the water as she did. "Does that annoy you?"

Brie gave him an odd, searching look. "Yes, of course. Just because I have no desire to rule doesn't mean the law itself isn't wrong. My grandfather was instrumental in bringing women's suffrage to Cordina. My own father has gone further by appointing women to positions of importance, but change is slow."

"Invariably."

"You're practical and patient by nature." She gave a

quick shrug. "I'm not. When change is for the better, I see no reason for it to creep along."

"You can't overlook the human element."

"Especially when some humans are too steeped in tradition to see the advantage of progress."

"Loubet."

Brie sent him an appreciative look. "I can see why my father enjoys having you around, Reeve."

"How much do you know about Loubet?"

"I can read," she said simply. "I can listen. The picture I gain is one of a very conservative man. Stuffy." She rose, stretching so that the bikini briefs went taut over her hips. "True, he's an excellent minister in his way, but so very, very cautious. I read in my diary where he tried to discourage me from my tour of Africa last year. He didn't feel it proper for a woman. Nor does he feel it proper for me to meet with the National Council over budget matters." Frustration showed briefly. She was, Reeve noted, learning fast. "If men like Loubet had their way, women would do no more than make coffee and babies."

"I've always been of the opinion that such things should be joint efforts."

She smiled down at him, obviously amused and relaxed. "But then, you're not such a traditionalist. Your mother was a circuit-court judge." At Reeve's steady look, her smile widened. "I did my homework," she reminded him. "You weren't a subject I overlooked. You graduated from American University summa cum laude. Under the current circumstances, I find it interesting that you have a degree in psychology."

"A tool," he said easily, "in the career I chose."

"True enough. After two and half years on the police force and three citations for bravery, you went undercover. The facts become vague there, but rumor has it that you were on the team responsible for breaking one of the major crime rings operating in and around the District of Columbia. There's also a rumor that at the request of a certain United States senator, you served on his security force. With your reputation, your intelligence and your record you could easily have made the rank of captain, despite your age. Instead you chose to resign from the force altogether."

"For someone who said they knew little about me, you certainly have enough data."

"That tells me nothing about you." She walked to starboard. "I want to cool off. Will you come?" Before he could answer, she was over the side and in the water.

She was unbelievably provocative, but he'd yet to determine if this was deliberate. Thoughtful, Reeve rose. Finding out might be an education in itself. As smoothly as Brie, he slipped into the water.

"Soft," she said as she treaded water lazily. She'd already been under and her hair was wet, sleeked back from her face. Dripping, struck by the sun, it was nearly copper. Without makeup, in the strong light her face was exquisite. She had the bone structure, the complexion, photographers strove to immortalize. As an image, Reeve mused while he floated in the cool water near her, she was flawless. And as an image, she intrigued him—as images intrigue any man.

It was the woman he hungered for. He had yet to resolve whether he could separate one from the other and have what he wanted. He'd worked in law enforcement too long not to understand that every act had consequences. For everything taken, certain payments had to be made. It was far from clear as yet what his payment would be.

"I'm told you use the pool every day," she began, tipping back to drench her hair again. "You're a strong swimmer?"

He put just enough power into his kick to keep afloat. "Yes."

"Perhaps I'll join you one morning. I'm beginning to catch up with my work enough to lose an hour or so a day. Reeve..." She cupped water in her hand, then let it fall back into the sea. "You know the AHC ball is only a few weeks away."

"I'd have to be deaf not to. There's hammering and confusion in the Grand Ballroom almost every day."

"Just a few necessities," she told him offhandedly. "I only mention it because I feel you should know as my…" Her gaze went automatically to the ring on her left hand. Though he watched her, Reeve couldn't read her expression. "As my fiancé," she continued, "you'll be expected to open the ball with me and, in a very real sense, host it."

He watched her hair float and spread on the surface of the water. "And?"

"You see, until then we can keep social engagements to a minimum. The kidnapping, though we're playing it down, is an excellent excuse to keep a low profile, as well as the engagement itself. The ball, however, will be a full scale event with a great deal of press, and many people. I wonder if my father took into consideration the social pressure you'd be under when he asked you to take this—position."

Reeve dipped lower in the water, moving closer to her, but not close enough to touch. "You don't think I can handle it?"

She blinked, then focused on him with a laugh. "I've no doubt you'll handle it beautifully. After all, Alexander admires your mind and Bennett your tailoring. You couldn't have a better endorsement."

It amused him. "And so?"

"It's simply that the longer this goes on, the larger the favor becomes. Even after the engagement's broken, you'll have to deal with the repercussions, perhaps for years."

He turned to float on his back, and closed his eyes. "Don't worry about it, Brie. I'm not."

"Perhaps that's why I do," she persisted. "After all, I'm the cause of it."

"No." His disagreement was mild. "Your kidnapper's the cause of it."

For a moment, she said nothing. After all, he'd given her the opening she'd been angling for. Though she wasn't sure if she should take it, she went ahead. "Reeve, I won't ask if you were a good policeman. Or if you're good as a private detective. Your record speaks for itself. But are you happy in your work?"

This time he fell silent. His eyes closed, he could feel the sun beat down on his face while the water lapped cool over his body. He was still hovering over those coals.

No one had ever asked him if he'd been happy in his work. In fact, he hadn't asked himself until recently. The answer had been yes. And no.

"Yeah. I get a certain satisfaction from my work. I

believed in what I was doing on the force. Now I only take a case if I believe in it."

"Then why aren't you investigating the kidnapping, instead of guarding me?"

He shifted positions until the water lapped up to his shoulders and he could see her. He'd wondered when she would ask. "I'm a private investigator, not a cop anymore. Either way, I wouldn't have any jurisdiction here."

"I'm not talking about rules and laws, but of inclinations."

"One of the most admirable—and annoying—things about you is your perception." He wondered how her hair would feel now, wet from the sea, and gave in to the urge to reach out to it. He wondered how she would react if she knew he'd been doing some quiet probing, some peering behind the curtain of protocol and drawing his own conclusions without filling her in. In chess, even a queen could be used as a pawn.

"Yeah, I've thought about it." He answered easily, as easily as he treaded water. "But until your father asks, I'm officially security. Just security."

She felt the slight tug where his fingers tangled in her hair. Barely, just barely, their legs brushed under the water. "And if I asked? Would you consider it then?"

He kept his hand on her hair, but her question distracted him. "What do you want, Brie?"

"Help. Between my father and Loubet, I know next to nothing about the status of the investigation. I'm being protected, Reeve. Both of them want to cocoon me, and I don't like it."

"So you want me to do some digging and fill you in?"

"I thought of doing it on my own, but, then, you have more experience. And…" She smiled at him then. "It isn't possible for me to make a move without your being there in any case."

"Found another use for me, Your Highness?"

With a brow lifted, she managed to look dignified while she was soaking wet. "It wasn't meant to be an insult."

"No, probably not." He let her go. Perhaps it was time to use her and be used by her in a more active sense. "I'll give it some thought."

She decided it would be more strategic to retreat than advance. "I'll have to be content with that." In three smooth strokes she was back at the boat and pulling herself over the side. "Shall we try some of the wine and cold chicken Nanny packed for us?"

Nimbly he dropped onto the deck and stood a moment as the water drained from him. "Does Nanny always take on kitchen duty for you?"

"She likes to. We're all still children to her."

"Okay, then. No use letting the food go to waste."

"Ah, practicality again." She picked up a towel, rubbing it briefly over her hair before she tossed it aside again. "Well, then, come down into the cabin and help me. I heard that we have apple tarts, as well." With water still beaded on her skin, she ducked down into the small cabin. "You seem very at home on a boat," she commented when he joined her.

"I used to do a lot of sailing with my father."

"Used to?" Brie drew the bottle of wine from the cooler and gave the label a nod of approval.

"There hasn't been as much time for it the past few years."

"But you're close to him?"

After a quick look, Reeve found a corkscrew and took the bottle from her. "Yes, I'm close to him."

"Is he like my father. I mean—" She heard the quiet pop of the cork and began to look for glasses. "Is he very dignified and brilliant?"

"Is that how you see your father?"

"I suppose." She was frowning a bit as he poured the wine. "And kind, yes, but controlled." She knew she had her father's love, but his country and his power came first. "Men like that must be, after all. So are you."

He grinned as he touched his glass to hers. "Dignified, brilliant or kind?"

"Controlled," she returned, giving him an even look

as she sipped. "You make me wonder what you're thinking when you look at me."

The wine was cool and dry on his tongue. "I think you know."

"Not entirely." She took another sip, but hoped he wouldn't know it was for courage. "I do know that you want to make love with me."

The sun slanted in the open cabin door and framed her. "Yes."

"I ask myself why." Brie lowered her glass but held it with both hands. "Do you want to make love with every woman you meet?"

Under different circumstances, he'd have thought she was teasing, but her question was as simple as it sounded. So was his answer. "No."

She managed a smile, though her nerves were beginning to jump. Was this how the game was played? she wondered. And was it a game she was trying to play? "Every other one, then?"

"Only if they meet certain requirements."

"Which are?"

He cupped her face with his hand again. "If they make me think of them first thing in the morning, even before I know what day it is."

"I see." She twisted the glass between her fingers.

They were damp from nerves but still steady. "Do you think of me first thing in the morning?"

"Are you looking for flattery, Gabriella?"

"No."

He tilted her head up just a little more. She didn't stiffen, didn't move away, but again he sensed she was braced—not so much wary as waiting. "What, then?"

"To understand. Not knowing myself or my past, I want to understand if I'm attracted to you or simply to the idea of being with a man."

That was blunt enough, he mused. Not particularly flattering, but blunt. He'd asked for it. When he took the wineglass from her to set it aside, he noticed her fingers were tense. It gave him some satisfaction. "And are you attracted to me?"

"Are you looking for flattery?"

Humor came into his eyes. Reeve saw her smile in response. "No." Lightly, briefly, he touched his lips to hers while they watched each other. "Apparently we're both looking for the same thing."

"Perhaps." She hesitated only a moment before she brought her hands to his shoulders. "Perhaps it's time we discover if we've found it."

It was the way he'd wanted it—away from the palace, away from the walls. There was only the lap of water against the boat, so quiet, so rhythmic it was barely there at all. The cabin was small and low. There were shadows; there was sunlight. They were alone.

It was the way he'd wanted it—yet Reeve found himself hesitating. She looked so delicate in this light. Delicate, and he'd agreed to protect her. What sort of objectivitity would he have left after they became lovers? Brie rose on her toes to touch her mouth to his again. Reeve felt the pleasure, the sweetness, the need ease through him and settle.

What sort of objectivity did he have now? he admitted. It had been no less than the truth when he'd spoken of thinking of her every morning.

"You're not so sure," Brie murmured as she brushed his cheek. Excitement was rising in her, quicker, freer than she'd anticipated. He had doubts, she realized. He had second thoughts. It relieved her, aroused her. How inadequate she would have felt if he'd been so sure and she'd been the only one with nerves. "I come to you without any past. For now, for this moment, let's forget either of us has a future. Just today, Reeve. Just an hour—or a moment."

He could give her that. He would give her that. Take just that. This time when their lips came together it wasn't lightly, wasn't briefly. When it's only for the moment, needs intensify. They drive; they compel. Passion pent up; passion held back. Passion set free.

It was only for the moment. They'd both agreed; they'd both decided. They'd both forgotten.

Bodies pressed, flesh to flesh. Mouths tasted. Hungry, so hungry. He felt her hands skim up his back, small and smooth with the nails oval and tidy again. First they brushed, then they gripped and held. Strength—it poured from her making it easy to forget the delicacy. Needs— hers throbbed against him, making it easy to forget logic, plans, decisions. Longings had no logic; there was no plan to passion. The scent of the sea was mild. Her perfume was heady. Swimming in both of them, Reeve drew her with him onto the neat, narrow bunk.

Brie felt the tiny ridges of the woven spread as her back pressed against it. He'd told her there would be no roses, no satin sheets for them. Nor did she want them. Illusions weren't important. Reality was what she'd been searching for. With him she'd find it.

Legs tangled, arms tight, they drove each other. Some journeys are fast, furious and uncontrollable. She no longer thought, have I felt this before? Now was all they had. Opening her eyes, she looked up at him. His face was close, shadowed. It filled her vision. Now was all she wanted.

She reached up to bring his mouth back to hers.

Sweetness. Perhaps rose petals growing hot and ripe in the sun would taste like this. Pungent, like wine mulled over an open fire. Intoxicating, like champagne just uncorked. The more he tasted, the more he understood the meaning of true greed. And when he touched, he understood obsession.

She was like a statue, finely crafted, lovingly polished. But she was flesh and blood. Under his hand she moved, she pulsed. A statue might be admired, revered, studied. He could do that as his gaze roamed, as his hands stroked. But it was the woman he wanted. And the woman, he realized, had little more patience than he.

On a moan of pleasure she rolled, pinning him beneath her so that she could touch as freely as he. Pounding inside her was a need so wild it had no form, no beginning. Perhaps that's why she didn't fight it. Neither did she have a beginning.

She wanted to draw in that rich, deep male taste. And she did. She wanted to see her hand, pale and feminine, against his tanned skin. And she did. The sensations it brought her were something she'd never be able to describe with cool, clear reason, but she recognized happiness.

When she felt the top of her bikini loosen there wasn't any self-consciousness, only pleasure. *Touch me.* Her mind hummed the words only an instant before they were obeyed.

Lost in each other, they twisted on the bunk, demanding as much as they gave, offering as quickly as taking. As his mouth followed after his hands, she arched, crying out in astonished delight. If there was more, she'd have more. But if this was everything, she'd need nothing else.

Had she known her body was so sensitive? Had he? Incredibly, he seemed to know just where she craved to be touched, where she longed to have his lips brush or linger. There would be no less for him.

Bold, confident, she yanked at his brief trunks until there was nothing between him and her hands. Excitement careened through her when he groaned, when he shuddered. When she felt the last dregs of civilization desert him.

He'd made love before. He could remember what it was to feel a woman's body, to bury himself in one. Why was it he couldn't remember anything like this? If needs had ever clawed at him this sharply before, he had no knowledge of it. She was filling him, overwhelming him. All at once, there was nothing else—no sea lapping, no sun streaming through a door, no subtle movement of a boat beneath. There was only Gabriella, strong, sleek and seductive. There was only Gabriella, and a desire so tangled with emotion he couldn't fight it. He couldn't fight what he didn't understand. Instead he gave himself to it, and to her.

She arched, with her fingers digging into him like spurs. He heard her gasp, felt her stiffen. Then she was going with him, racing with him. Neither knew nor cared who set the pace.

Perhaps only moments had passed. It seemed like only moments. They were still tangled together, damp flesh against damp flesh, fast heart against fast heart. She wasn't relaxed, but stunned. Perhaps, she thought as Reeve's breathing continued to come unsteadily against her ear, she'd never relax again. Certainly she'd never be the same again.

She looked at the sun coming into the cabin. The same sun. She heard and felt the motion of the sea. The same sea. But not the same Gabriella. Never the same, from this moment. Innocence was gone. It was only now that she could be certain she'd had it to lose. And it was only now, she realized, that she was sure she'd wanted to.

"So there was no one else," she murmured, thinking aloud.

He felt something twist inside him. Lying still, he closed his eyes until it eased. When he lifted his head, he saw that her eyes were heavy, but her skin had that glow that spoke of the aftermath of passion. And he saw, when he looked down at her, that he'd lost a great deal more than his objectivity.

His heart, which he'd always believed was very firmly in his possession, was hers. At that moment, he knew, she could break him in half with a careless word. So it was he who spoke almost carelessly.

"No, there was no one else. Do you want an apology?"

She wasn't sure how to react or how to respond. Did a man feel responsible when he'd taken a woman's innocence? How would she know? Maybe not responsible, she thought, but uncomfortable. She couldn't afford the luxury of showing just how that idea hurt. Instead she kept her eyes level and her voice calm. "No, I don't look for apologies. Do you?"

His tone didn't change, nor his expression. She could read nothing in either one. "Why would I?"

"I started this, Reeve. I'm well aware of that." She started to rise, but he held her in place.

"Regrets?"

Her chin came up, just a bit, but enough to show him her mood. "No. Have you?"

The first time she'd been with a man, he thought, and he'd started a stilted, foolish conversation for his own defense. She was entitled to some tenderness, some sweetness and some truth. He touched her face, just a fingertip along her cheek.

"How could I regret being given something beautiful?" He kissed her then, softly, lengthily. "How can I regret having made love to you when it's something I'm already thinking about doing again?"

Reeve saw her lips curve just before he shifted so that he could cradle her against him. When they started back to Cordina, he knew he'd have to begin thinking again, planning. If he was to help her…but not now. Not just yet.

Content, and finding she could indeed relax, Brie rested a hand over his heart. It put her engagement ring directly in her line of vision. In the shadowed light it didn't seem so stunning, so demanding. It seemed—almost—as if it belonged there. But it wasn't real, she told herself quickly. It wasn't anything more than a prop in a complicated game. Not real. She closed her eyes, settling her body against Reeve's.

No, the ring wasn't real, but this was, she thought as she let herself drift. This was real—for as long as it lasted.

Chapter 8

Nothing seemed to become easier, Brie thought as she walked down the wide, window-lined corridor toward the Grand Ballroom. There were paintings that any artist with a soul might have wept over. There was furniture that had been lovingly polished for centuries. She passed by without a glance.

Rather than simplifying with each day, life became more complicated. Hadn't Reeve told her life was never simple? It wasn't any use wishing he'd been wrong.

Nearly a week before, she'd lain beside him on a narrow little bunk, half dozing until they'd turned to each other again. And made love again. Didn't that make them lovers? she asked herself as she stopped by one of the windows. Weren't lovers supposed to be at ease with each other—continue to desire each other? Yet a week had passed. In that week, Reeve had been faultlessly polite, outwardly attentive. He'd even in his own way been kind. And he'd gone out of his way to avoid touching her.

Putting her hands on the sill, Brie looked down. The guards were changing. As she watched the quiet, rather charming procedure, she wondered if Reeve felt it was time her guard also changed. And what she'd do if he left.

Of course, she'd known all along she'd have to face the gossip. Their engagement was still top news, not only in Cordina and Europe, but in the United States, as well. It wasn't possible to leaf through a magazine without finding herself.

That was nothing, Brie told herself with a little shrug. Gossip came and went. Unconsciously she twisted the diamond on her finger. Yes, gossip wasn't important. But Reeve was—perhaps too important.

If she understood herself better, her life better, would she know how to deal with what was happening? Or should she be dealing with what wasn't happening? No, life wasn't simple.

Falling in love must be difficult enough when everything was normal, but when there were so many blank pages, so many responsibilities to be learned, it was more frightening than exhilarating.

He'd go back to his farm, she reminded herself. To his farm, to his country, to his life. She, her family and a handful of people who had to be trusted were already aware of that. Even if Reeve asked her, could she go? He wouldn't ask, she told herself, trying to accept it. After all, she was just one lover in his life, one woman, one incident. It couldn't be for him as it was for her, where he was the only one.

Responsibility. She closed her eyes a moment as she forced the word into her head. She had to think of her responsibilities and stop dreaming. There'd be no splashy wedding, no lovely white dress and veil that every designer in the world was hoping to make. There'd be no huge cake, no crossed swords. There'd be an end, and a polite goodbye. She had no right to wish differently. But she hadn't the strength not to.

When she turned, the figure across the wide corridor had her jolting back toward the windows.

"Alexander." Brie dropped the hand she'd pressed instinctively to her heart. "You frightened me."

"I didn't want to disturb you. You looked…" Unhappy, he wanted to say. Lost. "Thoughtful."

"I was watching the guards." The smile she gave him was the same polite one she gave to everyone. Everyone but Reeve. But unlike Alexander, she didn't notice. "They look so trim and handsome in their uniforms. I was on my way to the ballroom to make sure everything was in order. It's hard to believe there's so little time left before the ball and yet so much to be done. Nearly all the responses are in, so—"

"Brie, must you talk to me as if I were someone you had to be polite to?"

She opened her mouth, then shut it again. He'd described it perfectly. She couldn't deny it. "I'm sorry. It's still so awkward."

"I'd rather you didn't put on that well-rehearsed front with me." He was young, tall and unquestionably annoyed. "You don't seem to find it necessary with Reeve."

Brie's voice chilled. "I apologized once. I've no intention of giving you another apology."

"I didn't want the first one." He crossed over to her with the quick measured steps of a man who had to know where he was going. One day he'd rule; the path was already worn. Though he was taller, they met now, as they always had, on level ground. "What I want is for you to give your family the same consideration you do a stranger."

She was tired of guilt, smothered by it. Her voice held no apology, only a challenge. "Is that advice or an order?"

"No one's ever been able to give you an order," he snapped as the temper he'd been clinging to for weeks broke free. "No one's ever been able to give you advice, for that matter. If you could be trusted to behave, it wouldn't be necessary for us to call in outsiders."

"I don't think it's necessary to bring Reeve into this conversation."

"No?" He took her arm as he spoke, an old habit. "Just what's between the two of you?"

Her voice had chilled before. Now her eyes followed suit. "None of your business."

"Damn it, Brie, I'm your brother."

"So I'm told," she said slowly, forgetting in temper any hurt she might cause. "And my younger brother by a few years. I don't find it necessary to be accountable to you, or to anyone, for my personal life."

"I might be younger," Alexander said between his teeth, "but I'm a man, and I know what's in a man's mind when he looks at a woman the way the American looks at you."

"Alexander, you should stop referring to him as 'the American,' as though he were an inferior breed. And," she continued before he could respond, "if I didn't like the way Reeve looked at me, I'd put a stop to it. I'm capable of taking care of myself."

"If you were, none of us would have gone through that

agony a few weeks ago." He saw her pale, but anger carried him further. "You were abducted, held, hospitalized. For days we waited, prayed, sat helpless. Doesn't it occur to you that the rest of us went through hell? Maybe you don't remember us, maybe we mean nothing to you right now. But that doesn't change the way we feel."

"Do you think I like it?" Unexpectedly tears started. If she'd had any warning, she might have stopped them. "Don't you know how hard I'm trying to get back? Now you push me into a corner, criticizing, demanding, insulting."

Temper faded, to be replaced by guilt. He'd forgotten just how lost she'd looked when she'd stood by the window. "It's what I've always done," he said gently. "You used to say that I'd practice ruling Cordina by trying to rule you and Bennett. I'm sorry, Brie. I love you. I can't stop loving you until you're ready for it."

"Oh, Alex." She went to him, for the first time holding him against her. He was so tall, so straight, so driven. But this time she felt a certain pride in knowing this. It wasn't easy for her to wait until things were clear, nor would it be easy for a man like her brother. "Did we always argue a great deal?"

"Always." He tightened his hold for a moment, then kissed the top of her head. "Father used to say it was because we both thought we knew everything."

"Well, at least I can't claim that anymore." With a quick, cleansing breath, she drew away. "Please don't resent Reeve, Alex. I can't say I didn't in the beginning, but the point is he's making quite a sacrifice staying here, going through all these maneuvers, when he'd rather be in his own country."

"It's difficult." Alex put his hands in his pockets and looked out the window. "I know he's under no obligation and what he's doing is done as a favor. I like him, actually."

Brie smiled, remembering that Bennett had used the same phrase. "I thought you did."

"It's just that I don't think things like this should go out of the family. Loubet's bad enough, but unavoidable."

"Would you get angry if I said I'd rather have Reeve hovering around me than Loubet?"

For the first time she saw Alexander grin. It was fast and endearing. "I'd think you'd lost your mind if you said otherwise."

"Your Highness."

Both Alexander and Brie turned. Janet Smithers gave them each a faultless curtsy. "I beg your pardon, Prince Alexander, Princess Gabriella."

She was, as usual, flawlessly groomed, with her dark hair tidy in a chignon and her rather thin face touched by only the most discreet of cosmetics. Her diction was perfect, unaccented, clear. Her suit was classicly and cleanly cut. And, to Brie's eyes, boring. Janet Smithers was efficient, intelligent, quick and quiet. If she were in a room with more than four people, no one would notice her. Perhaps for that reason alone, Brie was driven to be kind to her.

"Did you need me for something, Janet?"

"You've had a phone call, Your Highness, from Miss Christina Hamilton."

"Miss…" Brie trailed off a moment as she struggled to put details with the name.

"You went to college with her," Alexander supplied, dropping a hand on Brie's shoulder. It struck him that he was explaining to her about her closest friend. His touch was gentle. "She's an American, the daughter of a builder."

"Yes, I've visited her in—Houston. The press is sure she'll be in my wedding party, if not the maid of honor." Brie thought back on the newspaper clipping she'd been provided. A tall, stunning woman with a mane of dark hair and wicked smile. "You said she phoned, Janet. Did she leave a message?"

"She requested that I locate you, Your Highness." Not by the slightest expression did Janet reveal her thoughts on the request. "I'm to tell you that she'll phone back at exactly eleven o'clock."

"I see." Amused, Brie looked at her watch. That gave her fifteen minutes. "Well, then, I'd best go down to my rooms. Janet, if you don't mind, could you check the ballroom for me and make notes on anything left undone? I'm afraid I won't have time now."

"Of course, Your Highness." She gave the same lifeless curtsy before she continued on down the corridor.

"What an extraordinarily uninteresting woman," Alexander commented when she was out of earshot.

"Alex," Brie murmured, reprimanding him automatically even while she agreed.

"I know her credentials are impeccable and her efficiency's unquestionable, but God, it must be a bore to have to deal with her every morning."

Brie made a little movement, half shrug. "It doesn't start the day with any stimulation. Still, I must have had a reason for hiring her."

"You said you wanted a single woman you wouldn't get so attached to. When Alice left—Janet's predecessor—you moped around for days."

"I certainly chose wisely, then." When Alex gave her another quick grin, she shrugged again. "I'd best go down before this phone call comes through." She didn't add that she wanted to take a quick look through the notes and refresh her memory on Christina Hamilton. But before she left, she held out her hand. "Friends?"

Alexander took her hand, but gave a mock bow over it. "Friends, but I'm still keeping an eye on the American."

"As you please," she said carelessly, and turned to walk down the corridor. Alex watched her until she turned the corner toward the staircase. Perhaps he'd have a little talk with Reeve MacGee, as well.

Once in her sitting room, Brie sat down on the love seat with a stack of notes. She'd taken them in detail from instructions given by Reeve and her secretary. They were alphabetized, neat and thorough. They had to be thorough. The words on paper were her only reference to the people she'd once known so well. If her amnesia was to remain a closely guarded secret, she couldn't make a foolish mistake.

Christina Hamilton, she mused as she found the two pages that would comprise her knowledge of a woman who'd once been her friend. They'd spent four years together at the Sorbonne in Paris. When Brie closed her eyes, she thought she could almost see Paris—rain-washed streets, mad traffic and lovely old buildings, dusty little shops and gardens that could break your heart with color. But she couldn't see Christina Hamilton.

Chris, Brie corrected, noticing the nickname. Chris had studied art and now owned a gallery in Houston. There was a younger sister, Eve, whom Chris had alternately praised and despaired of. There had been romances. Brie's brows lifted as she ticked off the names of men Chris had been involved with. But not involved enough to marry. At twenty-five, she remained single, a successful, independent artist and businesswoman. Brie felt a dull twinge of envy that came and went so quickly it nearly went unnoticed.

Interesting, she reflected. Had there been rivalry between them? She could be given facts, data, information, but no one could list feelings to her.

When her private line rang, Brie kept her notes in one hand while she reached for the phone with the other. "Hello."

"The least you can do when an old friend calls you from across the Atlantic is to be available."

She liked the voice instantly. It was warm, dry and somewhat lazy. This time the twinge Brie felt was one of regret for not being able to recognize her emotions. "Chris…" She hesitated, then went with instinct. "Don't you know royalty keeps busy hours?"

The laugh rewarded her, but Brie didn't relax. "You know that whenever your crown gets too heavy you can take a break in Houston. God knows I can always use an extra pair of hands at the gallery. How are you, Brie, really?"

"I…" Oddly she found herself wanting to pour out everything, anything. There was something so comforting in the faceless voice. Duty, she remembered. Obligation. "I'm fine."

"It's Chris, remember? Oh, God, Brie, when I read about the kidnapping, I nearly—" She broke off, and Brie barely heard the quiet oath. "I spoke with your father, you know. I wanted to come. He didn't think it would be the best thing for you."

"Probably not. I've needed time, but I'm glad you wanted to."

"I'm not going to ask you questions about it, love. I'm sure the best thing to do is forget it entirely."

Brie gave a quick, uncontrollable laugh. "That seems to be what I'm doing."

Chris waited a moment, not quite satisfied with Brie's reaction. Ultimately she let it pass. "I will ask you what the hell's going on over there in Camelot."

"Going on?"

"This secret, whirlwind romance that's now at the engagement point. Brie, I know you've always been discreet, but I can't believe you didn't say a word to me, not a word about Reeve MacGee."

"Well, I suppose I really didn't know what to say." That had the ring of truth, Brie thought bitterly. "Everything's happened so fast. The engagement wasn't set or even discussed until Reeve came out here last month."

"How does your father feel?"

Brie gave a wry smile, grateful she didn't have to guard her expression. "You could say he nearly arranged it himself."

"I can't say I disapprove. An American ex-cop—you always said you'd never marry anyone too suitable."

Brie smiled a little. "Apparently I meant it."

"Actually, I was beginning to think you'd never take the plunge. You've always been too clever about men for your own good. Remember that model in Professor Debare's class?"

"The male model?" Brie hazarded, and was rewarded by another long laugh.

"Of course. You took one look at that magnificent study in masculine perfection and dubbed him a shallow, vain opportunist. The rest of us were drooling over his pectoral muscles—then he took Sylvia for fifty thousand francs."

"Poor Sylvia," Brie murmured, lost.

"Ah, well, she could afford it. Anyway, Brie, I know you're busy. I've called to invite myself, and Eve, for a few days."

"You know you're always welcome," Brie said automatically while her mind raced. "You're coming for the ball. Can you stay over then?"

"That's the plan. I hope you don't mind me dragging

Eve along, but the girl's driving Daddy mad. Brie, the child wants to be an actress."

"Oh?"

"You know Daddy, all business. He just can't see one of his darling girls wearing greasepaint and costumes. Now if she wanted to be an agent... Anyway, I thought it might do them both good to be a few thousand miles apart for a week or so. So if you can find an extra couple of beds in that palace of yours..."

"We've always got the folding cots."

"I knew I could count on you. We'll fly in the day before the ball, then. I can give you a hand—and meet your betrothed. By the way, Brie, how does it feel to be in love?"

"It—" She looked down at the ring on her hand, remembered what could sweep through her at a touch, at a look. "It's not very comfortable, actually."

Chris laughed again. "Did you think it was going to be? Take care of yourself, darling. I'll see you soon."

"Goodbye, Chris."

After she'd hung up, Brie sat still for a moment. She'd pulled it off. Christina Hamilton hadn't suspected anything. Brie had been bright, cheerful—deceitful. On a surge of temper, Brie tossed her notes so that they scattered, floated, then fell. She continued to frown at them after she'd heard the discreet knock at her door.

No, she wouldn't pick them up, Brie decided. She'd leave them just where they were, just where they belonged. "Yes, come in."

"Excuse me, Your Highness." Janet entered the sitting room with her usual lack of fuss. "I thought you'd like to know that the ballroom is in order. The drapes are being rehung." Though she glanced down to the papers lying on the floor, she made no comment. "Did your call come through?"

"Yes. Yes, I spoke with Miss Hamilton. And you're welcome to relay to my father that she suspects nothing."

Janet kept her hands folded neatly in front of her. "I beg your pardon, Your Highness?"

"Are you actually going to try to tell me you don't report to him?" Brie demanded. She rose, guilt and despair pushing at her. "I'm well aware of how closely you watch me, Janet."

"Your welfare is our only concern, Your Highness." Janet's voice remained colorless; her hands remained folded. "If I've offended you—"

"The subterfuge offends me," Brie tossed back. "All of it."

"I know Your Highness must feel—"

"You don't know how I feel," Brie interrupted as she whirled around the room. "How can you? Do you remember your father, your brother, your closest friend?"

"Your Highness…" After a moment, Janet took a step closer. That kind of temper, that kind of emotion had to be handled gently. "Perhaps none of us really understands, but that doesn't mean we don't care. If there were anything I could do to help…"

"No." Calmer, Brie turned back. "No, nothing. I'm sorry, Janet. I've no business shouting at you."

The smile was slight and did little to change her expression. "But you had to shout at someone. I'd hoped that is, I'd thought that perhaps after you'd talked to an old friend you might begin to remember something."

"Nothing. Sometimes I wonder if I ever will."

"But the doctors are hopeful, Your Highness."

"Doctors. I've had my fill of them, I'm afraid. They tell me to be patient." With a sigh, she began to rearrange a vase of gardenias. "How can I be patient when I have nothing more than flashes of who I am, of what happened to me?"

"But you have flashes?" Again Janet stepped closer, and after a brief hesitation laid a hand on Brie's. "You do remember bits and pieces?"

"No—impressions. Nothing as solid as pieces." The image of the knife was solid, and too ugly to dwell on. She needed something her mind could accept, something that eased it. "Pieces could be put together, couldn't they, Janet?"

"I'm not a doctor, Your Highness, but perhaps you should accept what you have now."

"That my life began less than a month ago?" Brie shook her head. "No, I can't. I won't. I'll find the first piece."

A floor above, Alexander sat in his cool-colored, spacious office and watched Reeve. He'd planned the interview carefully, and felt fully justified.

"I appreciate your giving me some time, Reeve."

"I'm sure you feel it's important, Alex."

"Gabriella's important."

Reeve nodded slowly. "To all of us."

It wasn't precisely the response he'd expected. Then again, he knew the value of having alternate moves. "While I appreciate what you're doing, Reeve, I feel my father leaned too heavily on an old friendship. Your position becomes more delicate every day."

Reeve sat back. Though there were nearly ten years between them, he didn't consider that he was facing a boy. Alexander had become a man earlier than most. Reeve debated his next move, and decided on an aggressive one. "Are you concerned about the possibility of my becoming your brother-in-law, Alex?"

If there was anger, the prince concealed it. "We both know what games are being played. My concern is

Gabriella. She's very vulnerable now, too vulnerable. Since, through my father's wishes, you remain closer to Gabriella than her family, you're in a position to observe and advise."

"And you're worried that I might observe what's none of my business and advise what's inappropriate."

Alexander spread his hands on his desk. "I can see why my father admires you, Reeve. And I think I can understand why Brie trusts you."

"But you don't."

"No, actually, I think I do." He wasn't unsure of himself. A man in Alexander's position couldn't afford to be. But he took a moment, anyway. He wanted to be certain he used the right words, the right tone. "I'm confident that as far as Brie's safety goes, she's in good hands. Otherwise…" He brought his gaze to Reeve's. They held level. "Otherwise, I'd see that you were either sent on your way or carefully watched."

"Fair enough." Reeve took out a cigarette. Alex shook his head at the offer. "So you're satisfied with my position as bodyguard, but you're concerned about a more personal relationship."

"You're aware that I objected—no, let's be candid— that I fought the business of your becoming engaged to my sister."

"I'm aware that both you and Loubet expressed doubts."

"I don't like my opinion coinciding with Loubet's," Alexander muttered, then gave Reeve a quick, completely open smile. "My father considers Loubet's talents and experience as minister of state compensation for his outdated views on a great number of things."

"Then there's the matter of the limp." At Alexander's expression, Reeve blew out a stream of smoke. "A great deal of our families' histories are known to each other, Alex. My father happened to be in the car along with Loubet and the prince when they had the accident some thirty-five years ago. Your father broke his arm, mine suffered a mild concussion. Loubet, unfortunately, had more serious injuries."

"The accident has nothing to do with Loubet's position now."

"No, I'm quite sure it doesn't. Your father doesn't handle things that way. But perhaps he's more tolerant because of it. He was driving. A certain amount of remorse is only human. In any case—" Reeve brushed the subject aside "—it merely serves to show that our families are tied in certain ways. Old friendships, old bonds. My engagement to your sister was easily accepted because of that."

"Do you easily accept it?"

This time it was Reeve who hesitated. "Alex, do you want a comfortable answer or the truth?"

"The truth."

"It wasn't a simple matter for me to agree to a mock engagement to Gabriella. It isn't a simple matter for me to go through the motions of being her fiancé, or to see my ring on her finger. It isn't simple," Reeve said slowly, "because I'm in love with her."

Alexander didn't speak, nor did hc give any sign of surprise. After a moment, he reached out and ran a fingertip down a silver picture frame. His sister looked back out at him, smiling and lovely. "What do you intend to do about it?"

Reeve lifted a brow. "Isn't it your father's place to ask, Alex?"

"It isn't my father you've told."

"No." Reeve crushed out his cigarette slowly, deliberately. "I don't intend to do anything about it. I'm well aware what my responsibilities and my limitations are as concerns your sister."

"I see." Alexander picked up a pen and ran it absently through his fingers. It seemed he didn't know Reeve MacGee as well as he'd thought. "And Brie's feelings?"

"Are Brie's feelings. She doesn't need any more complications at this point. Once she remembers, she'll no longer need me."

"Just like that?"

"I'm a realist. Whatever develops between Brie and me now is very likely to change once her memory returns."

"And yet you want to help her get to that point."

"She needs to remember," Reeve said evenly. "She suffers."

Alex looked at the picture again, was drawn to it. "I know that."

"Do you? Do you know how guilty she feels that she can't remember the people who want her love? Do you know how frightened she is when she has one of the dreams that take her to the edge of remembering, then leave her lost?"

"No." Alexander dropped the pen. "She doesn't confide in me—I think I see why. And I think I see why my father trusts you completely." Looking down at his hands, he felt helpless, frustrated. "She has dreams?"

"She remembers the dark, hearing voices, being afraid." He thought of her dream about the knife, but kept his silence there. That was for Brie to tell. "It seems to be little more than that."

"I see. I understand a great deal more now." Again Alexander's gaze locked on his. "You've a right to resent my questions, Reeve, but I've the right to ask them."

"We'll agree to both of those." Rising, Reeve put an

end to the interview himself. "Just remember, I'll do everything I'm capable of doing to keep your sister safe."

Alex stood to face him. "We can both agree to that, as well."

It was late when Reeve stood under a hot, soothing shower. He needed it more than he needed an empty bed. His evening had been spent escorting Brie to a dinner party, where they'd both been deluged with questions on the wedding. When, who, where? How much? How soon? How many?

If things didn't begin to turn around for Brie after the ball, they'd no longer be able to use preparations for that as an excuse for the lack of plans.

All they needed now was a fictitious wedding date, Reeve thought, letting water pour over his head and beat on his neck. If things didn't begin to jell soon, they'd find themselves standing at the altar just to keep the tongues from wagging.

That would be the ultimate in fantasy and foolishness, wouldn't it? he asked himself. Married to prevent rumors from generating. Yet how much more difficult could that be than what was going on now?

He'd had to sit through dinner, watching her, being congratulated on his good fortune. He'd had to sit within a few feet of her and remember what it had been like for them when they'd just been two people on a narrow bunk in a tiny cabin.

Trouble was, he remembered too well, needed too much. Since then he'd been very careful to avoid any opportunity for them to be quite that alone. When they weren't in the palace or in the car, they were at a party or one of her charity functions. He took her to the AHC headquarters or the Red Cross. He accompanied her to the museum, but he never suggested another sail.

Neither of them could afford it, he decided as he stepped from the shower. Certainly neither of them had planned on his forgetting the rules and falling in love with her. He still had a job to do. She still had a life to rediscover. Once both were accomplished, the ties would be broken.

As they should be, Reeve thought. With a towel hooked around his waist, he rubbed a fresh one over his hair. Brie didn't belong in a ramshackle farmhouse in the mountains. He didn't belong in a palace. It was as simple as that.

Then he stepped through to the bedroom and nothing was simple.

Brie sat in an armchair, a low light shining over her shoulder as she thumbed through a book. The nerves were there, but so was determination. She managed to hide the first as she looked up.

"I think I've always loved Steinbeck," she said as she set the book aside. "He makes me feel as though I've been to Monterey." She rose, and though she'd been too nervous to plan it, she looked like a bride. The simple white robe fell to her ankles and covered her arms to the wrist. Her hair fell over her shoulders, where lace gave a glimpse of the skin beneath.

Reeve stood where he was, as stunned by the ache as he'd ever been stunned by anything. "Did you want to borrow a book?"

"No." She stepped toward him as though she were confident. "You wouldn't come to me, Reeve. I thought it was time I came to you." Needing the contact, she took his hands. Somehow it made the confidence genuine. "You can't send me away," she murmured. "I won't go."

No, he couldn't send her away. Common sense might tell him to, but common sense hadn't a chance. "Pulling rank again, Gabriella?"

"Only if I must." She lifted his hand to her face a moment. "Tell me you don't want me. I might hate you for it, but I won't make a fool of myself again."

He knew he could lie, and that the lie might be best for her. But the lie wouldn't come. "I can't tell you I don't want you. I doubt I could tell you even if I thought I could make you believe it. And I'm very likely to make a fool of myself."

With a smile, she wrapped her arms around him. "Hold me. Just hold me." She closed her eyes as her cheek pressed against his shoulder. This was where she'd wanted to be. "I've been going crazy waiting, wondering. I nearly lost my nerve tonight coming down the hall."

"It might have been best if you had. It's hardly discreet for you to visit me in my room at midnight."

Laughing, she tossed her head back. "No, it's not. So let's make the best of it."

With her arms flung around his neck, she found his mouth with hers. It was what she wanted, all she wanted, Brie realized as she poured herself into the kiss. Whatever she had to fight to get another day successfully behind her, if she could share the night with him, she could do it.

"Reeve." Slowly she drew away so that she could see him. "For tonight, let's not have any pretenses, any deceptions." She brought his hand to her face again, but this time she pressed her mouth to it. "I need you. Can that be enough?"

"It's enough." He loosened the sash of her robe. "Let me show you."

The light was low, the windows open. She could smell the sweet peas that climbed gleefully on the trellis just below. When he slipped the robe from her shoulders, she shivered. But from excitement, not from the breeze.

"You're lovely, Brie." Now that they were bare, Reeve followed the slope of her shoulders with his hands. "Every time I see you, it's like the first time. The light is different, the angle, but it strikes me just as it did the first time."

He brushed her hair back from her face until only his hand framed it. Then he watched her, only watched, until her heart began to thud. He kissed her, once, twice, slowly but lightly. As her lids fluttered closed, he brushed his lips over them, as well. Gentleness he hadn't shown before. She'd come to him. Now he could give it.

When he lifted her in his arms, her eyes opened in surprise. She hadn't expected an old-fashioned, romantic gesture from him. There was much more he had to give that she hadn't expected.

They lay together on the bed, naked, needing. But he brought her fingers to his lips, kissing them one by one. When she reached for him he lowered to her, but only for slow kisses, light caresses. Unlike the first time, this fire only smoldered, half tormenting, half delighting.

She'd thought he'd already shown her every point of pleasure her body was capable of. Now he showed her more, exquisitely.

Brie knew there was a restlessness in him. A violence. The first time they'd loved, she'd felt it, sensed it, wanted it. Tonight he brought none of it with him. This night was tender. Tenderness that brought a heavy, misty plea-sure she hadn't explored. This excitement was different, drifting, not soothing but sweet. She gave herself to it, willing, for the moment, to be led.

He'd taken her innocence. In some strange way Reeve was aware that she'd given a portion of his back to him. It hadn't been something he'd looked for or wanted, nor was it something he could have prevented. Perhaps one day, when their lives separated and he had to deal with what he'd had and what he'd lost, he'd resent it. Tonight, when she was close, soft, giving, he only treasured it.

So he went slowly, gently. What passed between them this night would be something neither of them would ever be able to forget.

He nibbled, finding the long narrow bone of her hip fascinating. He knew just how strong she was. After all, he'd followed her through days of work and demands and evenings that were social, but equally taxing. Yet just there her skin was so fragile, so sensitive. She had the small, delicate body of a woman who lived her life in luxury. But she had the mind, he knew, of a woman who never took one moment of it for granted.

Is that why he loved her? Did it matter?

She could only sigh as his mouth traced lower, lower down her body. He was taking her places she'd never imagined. This world was dark, but there was no fear.

Just anticipation. It drummed through her, to be joined by arousal, pleasure, satisfaction. One layered on top of the other.

There were night birds calling to each other, but the murmur of her name on Reeve's lips seemed sweeter. The breeze whispered across her face, but his breath, skimming across her skin was warmer. The sheets were soft, cool only until they were touched with flesh that quickly warmed them. If she let her eyes open, she could see her own hand stroke over him. And triumph in it.

His tongue traced, teased, lingered, then invaded. Suddenly she was catapulted out of the dark, soothing world and into the light.

She wasn't aware that her fingers gripped her bed-sheets as she arched. She wasn't aware that she called out his name mindlessly. But she was aware, all at once, that pleasure could be almost too much to bear. She knew, as he drew from her relentlessly, that he was giving to her, as well. Everything, all things, were there for her to take if only she had the strength. She'd find it.

Quiet thoughts vanished. Turbulent ones tumbled into her. To have him—completely, enduringly. To know that he was rocked by the power even as she was. To feel the shudder that told her he, too, was overwhelmed. That was enough to both ensure survival and to make survival unimportant. Though she trembled, dazed, he didn't give her time to catch her breath before he drove her up and beyond again.

Then, when she thought there could be no more, he took her with all the fierce need he'd kept harnessed.

Chapter 9

Brie knew she shouldn't have stayed with him through the night, but she found she wanted, needed, to sleep with him, even if it were only for a few hours. It had been so easy in the dark, quiet night to forget discretion and to take what lovers are entitled to. It had been so sweet to drift off to sleep with her hand caught in his. If in the morning there were consequences, they'd be worth those few hours.

It was Reeve who awoke first and roused her just before dawn when the light was gray and indistinct. This was the time between, when the night birds began to sleep and the lark awakened. Brie felt the light kiss on her shoulder, and merely sighed and snuggled closer.

The nip on her earlobe made her shudder—but lazily, comfortably.

"Brie, the sun's coming up."

"Mmmm. Kiss me again."

He kissed her again, this time on the lips, until he was sure she was awake. "The servants will be up and around soon," he told her as her eyes half opened. "You shouldn't be here."

"Worried about your reputation again?" She yawned and wrapped her arms around his neck.

Reeve grinned and comfortably cupped her breast. She made him feel so…at home. Had he just noticed it? "Naturally."

Pleased with herself, she twined his hair around her finger. "I suppose I've compromised you."

"You did come to my room, after all. How could I risk refusing a princess?"

She arched a brow. "Very wise. So…" She touched her tongue to her top lip. "If I commanded you to make love with me again, right now—"

"I'd tell you to get your buns out of bed." He kissed her before she could object. "Your Serene Highness."

"Very well," she said loftily, and rolled aside. She stood, naked, and shook back her hair. He thought then that she was no Sleeping Beauty just coming to life, but a woman who already knew and accepted her own power. "Since you cast me aside so easily, you'll have to come to me next time." She picked up her discarded robe, but took her time about putting it on. "That is, unless you'd like to be tossed in the dungeons. They are, I'm told, very deep, dank and dark."

He watched her slide one arm in a sleeve. "Blackmail?"

"I've no conscience." She drew on the other sleeve, then slowly crossed and tied the robe.

No, she was no Sleeping Beauty, he thought again. She was a woman who deserved more than promises. "Brie…" Reeve sat up, pulling a hand through his hair. "Alexander and I had a talk yesterday."

Brie kept her hands on the sash, though they were no longer relaxed. "Oh? About me, I assume."

"Yes, about you."

"Well?"

"That royal tone doesn't work on me, Brie. You should know that by now."

As if it were vital, she smoothed out the satin of the sash. "What does?"

"Honesty."

She looked back at him, then sighed. It was an answer she should have expected. "All right, then. Alex and I did our own share of talking—arguing—yesterday. I can't say I appreciate the two of you getting together for a chat about me and my welfare."

"He's concerned. I'm concerned."

"Is that an excuse for everything?"

"It's a reason for everything."

Her breath came out slowly. "I'm sorry, I don't mean to be unfair, Reeve. I don't, though it might appear differently, even mean to be ungrateful. It just seems as though while everyone's so concerned, so worried, everyone continues to make demands." She began to walk as she spoke—to the window and away, to the mirror and back again, as if she weren't quite ready to face herself that morning. "They want me to go along with Loubet's plan about covering up the amnesia so that there's no panic and the investigation can go on quietly. They want you and me to go on with this deception about being engaged. I think—I'm beginning to think that bothers me most of all."

"I see."

She glanced up, unsmiling. "I wonder if you can," she murmured. "On one hand I get sympathy, concern, and on the other, obligations."

"Is there something you'd rather do? Some way you'd rather try?"

"No." She shook her head. "No. What did Alexander conclude, then?"

"He decided to trust me. Have you?"

She looked at him in surprise, then realized how she must have appeared. "You know I trust you. I wouldn't be here with you if I didn't."

He made the decision instantly. Sometimes it was the best way. "Can you clear your schedule today and come with me?"

"Yes."

"No questions?"

She moved her shoulders. "All right, if you want one. Where?"

"To the little farm." He waited for her reaction, but she only watched him. "I think it's time we worked together."

She closed her eyes a moment, then crossed to the bed. "Thank you."

He felt his emotions rise and tangle again. They always would, he realized, with her. "You might not be grateful later."

"Yes, I will." Bending, she kissed him, not in passion, but in friendship. "No matter what."

The corridors were dim when she left Reeve's room to go to her own. But her spirit wasn't. She had hope again. This wouldn't be a day where she just followed the schedule that had been set for her. Today, at last, she'd do something to bring the past and present together. Perhaps the key was at the little farm. Perhaps with Reeve's help she'd find it.

Quietly Brie opened the door to her bedroom, anxious to begin. Humming a little, she walked to the windows and began pushing aside the curtains so light could spill in.

"So."

She jolted, whirled, then swore under her breath. "Nanny."

The old woman straightened in the chair and gave Brie a long, steady look. If her bones were stiff, she gave no sign. Brie felt the patience, the disapproval, and felt the blood creep into her cheeks.

"Well you should blush, young lady, tiptoeing into your room with the sun."

"Have you been here all night?"

"Yes. Which is more than you can say." Nanny tapped a long, curved fingernail against the arm of the chair. She saw the change, but, then, she'd seen it days before when Brie had come back from sailing. When a woman was old, she was still a woman. "So you decided to take a lover. Tell me, are you pleased with yourself?"

Defiant, and amazed that she felt the need to be, Brie lifted her chin. "Yes."

Nanny studied her—the tumbled hair, the flushed

cheeks and the eyes where the echo of passion remained. "That's as it should be," she murmured. "You're in love."

She could have denied it. It was on the tip of her tongue to do so, when she realized it would be a lie. Just one more lie. "Yes, I'm in love."

"Then I'll tell you to be careful." Nanny's face looked old and pale in the morning light, but her eyes were ageless. "When a woman's in love with her lover, she risks more than her body, more than her time. You understand?"

"Yes, I think I do." Brie smiled and moved over to kneel at Nanny's feet. "Why did you sleep all night in a chair instead of your bed?"

"Perhaps you've taken a lover, but I still look after you. I brought you warm milk—you don't sleep well."

Bric looked over and saw the thick cup on the table. "And I worried you because I wasn't here." She brought the woman's hard little hand to her cheek. "I'm sorry, Nanny."

"I suspected you were with the American." She sniffed a little. "A pity his blood isn't as blue as his eyes, but you could do worse."

The diamond weighed heavily on her finger. "It's still just a dream, isn't it?"

"You don't dream enough," Nanny said briskly. "So

I brought you milk and found you'd looked for a different kind of comfort."

This time Brie laughed. "Would you scold me if I said I much preferred it?"

"I'd simply advise you to keep your preferences from your father for a while yet." Nanny's voice was dry and amused as Brie grinned up at her. "Perhaps you have no more use for the other comfort I brought you." Reaching beside her, she pulled out a plain, round-faced rag doll in a tattered pinafore. "When you were a child and were restless in the night, you'd reach for this."

"Poor ugly thing," Brie murmured as she took it in her hands.

"You called her 'Henrietta Homely.'"

"I hope she didn't mind," Brie began as she ran a hand over the doll's hair. Then she went stiff and very still.

A young girl in a small bed with pink hangings, pink sheets, pink spread. White frills on a vanity table. Rosebuds on the wallpaper. Music drifting up from far away. A waltz, slow and romantic. And there was a woman, the woman from the portrait, smiling, murmuring, laughing a little as she leaned over the bed, so that the emeralds in her ears caught the low light. Her dress was like the emeralds, green and rich. It rustled musically as the best of silks do. She smelled of apple blossoms, of spring, of youth.

"Gabriella." Nanny put a hand to Brie's shoulder and squeezed. Beneath the thin robe, she could feel the skin, icy. "Gabriella."

"My room," Brie whispered as she continued to stare down at the doll. "My room when I was a girl—what color?"

"Pink," Nanny said haltingly. "It was all pink and white, like a pastry."

"And my mother." Brie's fingers dug into the rag doll, but she didn't know it. Sweat pearled on her forehead, but she didn't know that, either. As long as she pushed, as long as she held on, she could see and remember. "Did she have a green silk dress? Emerald green. A ball gown?"

"Strapless." With an effort, the old woman kept her voice calm and quiet. "The waist was very snug. The skirt was very full."

"And her scent was like apple blossoms. She was so beautiful."

"Yes." Nanny's strong fingers held her shoulder firmly. "Do you remember?"

"I—she came to see me. There was music, a waltz playing. She came to tuck me in."

"She would always. First you, then Alexander, then

Bennett. Your father would come up if he could slip away, but they'd both come to the nursery before they went to bed. I'll go get your father now."

"No." Brie pressed the doll close. She couldn't hold the image any longer. It left her weak and breathless. "No, not yet. That's all there is. Just that one picture, and I need so much more. Nanny..." Eyes brimming, Brie looked up again. "I did love her. Finally I can feel it. I loved her so much. Now, remembering that, it's like losing her again."

With her old nurse stroking her hair, Brie lay down her head and wept. The bedroom door opened no more than a crack, then shut soundlessly.

"So you're going for a ride in the country."

Brie stood in the main hall, looking at her father. Her face was carefully made up. The signs of weeping were gone. But her nerves weren't as easily concealed. She twisted the strap of the purse she wore over her shoulder.

"Yes. I told Janet to cancel my appointments. There wasn't anything very important—a fitting, some paperwork at the AHC that I can see to just as easily tomorrow."

"Brie, you don't have to justify taking a day off to me." Though he wasn't certain how he'd be received, Armand took her hand. "Have I asked too much of you?"

"No—" She shook her head. "I don't know."

"Never has it been more difficult for me to be both ruler and father. If you asked..." His fingers tightened briefly on her hand. "If you wanted, Gabriella, I'd take you away for a few weeks. A cruise, perhaps, or just a trip to the cottage in Sardina."

She couldn't remind him that she didn't know the cottage in Sardina. Instead she smiled. "There's no need. Dr. Franco must have told you that I'm strong as a horse."

"And Dr. Kijinsky tells me that you're still troubled by images, dreams."

Brie took a breath and tried not to regret that she'd finally told the analyst everything. "Some things take longer to heal."

He couldn't beg her to talk to him as he knew she talked to Reeve. Such things had to come from the heart. Yet neither could he forget how often she'd curl into his lap, her head on his shoulder, as she poured out her feelings.

"You look tired," he murmured. "The country air will do you good. You're going to the little farm?"

She kept her eyes level. She wouldn't be turned away from what she had to do. "Yes."

He saw the determination, respected it. Feared it. "When you come back, will you tell me whatever you remember, whatever you felt?"

For the first time her hand relaxed in his. "Yes, of course." For his sake, for the sake of the woman in the emerald dress who'd tucked her in, Brie stepped forward to brush his cheek with her lips. "Don't worry about me. Reeve will be there."

Struggling not to feel replaced, Armand watched her walk down the long length of the hall. A footman opened the door wide, and she stepped into the sunshine.

For a long time Reeve said nothing. He drove at an easy speed along the winding, climbing, dipping coast road. Turmoil. It was quickly recognized, though the source wasn't. He could wait.

The city of Cordina was left behind, then the port of Lebarre. Now and then they'd pass a cottage where the gardens were carefully tended and the flowers bloomed in profusion. This was the road where she'd run that night, escaping. He wondered if she realized it.

She saw nothing familiar, nothing that should make her tense. But she was tense. The land was lovely in its windswept, rock-tumbled way. It was quiet, colorful, idyllic. Yet she continued to worry the strap of her bag.

"Do you want to stop, Gabriella? Would you rather go somewhere else?"

She turned to him quickly, then just as quickly turned away again. "No. No, of course not. Cordina's a beautiful country, isn't it?"

"Why don't you tell me what's wrong?"

"I'm not sure." She made her hand lie still in her lap. "I feel uneasy, as if I should be looking over my shoulder."

He'd already decided to give her whatever answers she needed without frills or cushions. "You ran along this road a month ago. In a storm."

Her fingers curled. She made them relax. "Was I running toward the city or away?"

He glanced at her again. It hadn't occurred to him to make that particular connection. His respect for her mind went up another notch. "Toward. You were no more than three miles outside of Lebarre when you collapsed."

She nodded. "Then I was lucky, or I still knew enough to go in the right direction. Reeve, this morning..."

Regrets? he wondered as his fingers tightened on the wheel. Were regrets and common sense coming so soon? "What about it?"

"Nanny was waiting for me in my room."

Should he be amused? Whether he should or not, Reeve couldn't prevent the smile at the picture that formed in his mind. "And?"

"We talked. She brings warm milk to me some nights. I suppose I wasn't thinking of such things last night." Brie smiled, too, but only briefly. "She also brought me a doll, something I'd had as a child." Slowly, determined to be very clear on every detail, Brie told him what she'd remembered. "That was all," she said at length. "But this time it wasn't an impression, it wasn't a dream. I remembered."

"Have you told anyone else?"

"No."

"You'll tell Kijinsky when you see him tomorrow." It wasn't a question but more in the line of an order. Brie struggled not to feel resentment but to understand.

"Yes, of course. Do you think it's a beginning for me?"

He'd slowed the car while she'd talked. Now he sped up again. "I think you're getting stronger. That was a memory you could handle, maybe one you needed before you faced the rest."

"And the rest will come."

"The rest will come," he agreed. And when it did, she wouldn't need him any longer. His job would be over. His farm…

He thought of it now, but it seemed as if he'd been away years rather than weeks. It didn't seem merely a quiet, serene spot any longer, but lonely, empty. When he went back, he'd no longer be the same man with the same desires.

Following the directions he'd been given, Reeve turned off the coast road and headed away from the sea. The going wasn't as smooth here. Again he slowed the car, this time because of the uneven road.

Before long, the trees muffled, then silenced the sound of water. The hills were greener, the landscape less dramatic. They heard a dog bark, a cow moo low and deep. He could almost imagine he was going home.

He turned again, doubling back a bit on a road that was no more than dirt and stone. Then a field stretched out on one side, green and overgrown. Trees grew thick on the other.

"This is it?"

"Yes." Reeve turned off the ignition.

"They found my car here?"

"That's right."

She sat for a moment, waiting. "Why do I always expect it to be easy?" she said. "Somehow I think that when I see something, when I know something, it'll be clear. It never really is. But there are times I feel the knife in my hand." She glanced down at her palm. "I can feel it, and when I do, I know I'm capable of killing."

"We all are, under the right circumstances."

"No." Outwardly calm, Brie folded her hands. Agony was kept inside, where she had been taught personal agonies belonged. "I don't believe that. To kill, to take a life, requires an understanding, an acceptance of violence. A dark side. In some, it's strong enough to over-power every other instinct."

"And what would have happened to you if you'd closed your eyes and rejected violence?" He gripped her shoulder harder than was necessary and made her face him. "Blessed are the passive, Brie? You know better."

He pulled out her emotions with a look. She couldn't stop it. "I don't want violence in my life," she said passionately. "And I don't, I won't, accept the fact that I've killed."

"Then you'll never pull out of this." His voice was harsh as he backed her into the seat. "You'll go on living your fantasy. The princess in the castle—cool, distant and unattainable."

"You speak to me of fantasy?" He was pushing her; it no longer mattered that she'd once asked him to. He was pushing her toward a dark boundary. "You make your own illusions. A man who's spent his life looking for trouble, seeking it out, who pretends he'll be content to sit on the porch and watch his crops grow."

She'd hit the mark. Fury and frustration welled up and poured out in his voice. He had his fantasies, and she'd become one of them. "At least I know what my own reality is and I've faced it. I need the farm for reasons you're not willing to understand. I need it because

I know what I'm capable of, what I've done and what I might do yet."

"With no regrets."

"Damn regrets. But tomorrow might be different. I have a choice." He wanted to believe it.

"You do." Suddenly weary, she looked away. "Perhaps that's where we differ. How can I live my life the way I'm obligated to live it knowing that I'm—"

"Human," he interrupted. "Just like the rest of us."

"You simplify."

"Are you going to tell me that a title makes you above the rest of us?"

She started to snap, then let out a long breath. "You've cornered me. No, I'm human, and flawed, and I'm afraid. Accepting my own…shadows seems the most difficult of all."

"Do you want to go on?"

"Yes." She reached for the door handle. "Yes, I want to go on." Stepping from the car, she looked around and wished she knew where to begin. Perhaps she already had. "Have you come out here before?"

"No."

"Good, then it's like the first time for both of us." She shielded her eyes, looking. "It's so quiet. I wonder if I planned to have the fields planted one day."

"You talked of it."

"But did nothing about it." She began to walk.

Wildflowers grew as they pleased, in the field, along the path. Some were yellow, others blue. Fat, business-like bees hummed around them. She saw a butterfly as big as the palm of her hand land and balance on a petal. The air smelled of grass, rich grass, rich dirt. She walked on without purpose.

A jay swooped by, annoyed by the intrusion. It flew off, complaining, into the trees. No fairy tale here, she mused. It would be hard, hard work to clear, to plant, to harvest. Is that why it remained undone? Had she only been dreaming again?

"Why did I buy this?"

"You wanted a place of your own. You needed a place where you could get away."

"Escape again?"

"Solitude," he corrected. "There's a difference."

"But it needs a house." Suddenly impatient, she turned in a circle. "It needs to live. Look there—if some of those trees were cleared, a house could snuggle in and look out over the fields. There'd be stables there. Yes, and a pasture. A hen house, too." Caught up, she walked farther, quickly. "Right along here. A farm has to have fresh eggs. There should be dogs and children, don't you see? It's nothing without them. Daisies in a windowbox.

Laughter through the doorways. The land shouldn't sit unloved this way."

He could see it as she did. After all, he'd seen his own land in precisely the same way. Yet they remained worlds apart. "From what I've been told, it isn't unloved."

"But untended. Nothing alive can go untended."

Annoyed with herself, she turned to walk farther in the high grass. As she did, her foot hit something and set it rattling against rock. Reeve bent down and picked up a red thermos, empty, with the stopper and top missing. His instincts began to hum. He held it by the base, touching no more than was necessary. He'd been a cop too long.

"In your dreams you're sitting someplace quiet, drinking coffee from a red thermos."

Brie stared at it as though it were something vile. "Yes."

"And you were sleepy." Casually he sniffed at the opening, but his mind was already working ahead. Just how sophisticated was the police lab in Cordina? he wondered. And why hadn't the farm been thoroughly investigated? Why had a piece of evidence so potentially important been left unheeded? He was damn well going to find out.

She'd walked this way on her own, he mused. He'd been very careful not to influence her direction. Then she systematically pointed out where a house, the stables would be. If she'd sat here before… He skimmed until his gaze rested on a big, smooth rock. It was only a few yards away, where the sun would be full and warm in the late morning and early afternoon. A spot for a dreamer.

Yes, if she'd sat there, resting, thinking, drinking coffee—

"What are you thinking?"

He brought his gaze back to her. "I'm thinking you may have sat against that rock there, drinking your coffee, planning. You got sleepy, perhaps even dozed off. But then you tried to shake the sleepiness off. You told me that in your dreams you didn't want to be sleepy. So maybe you managed to get up, stumble in the direction of your car." Turning, he looked back to where his sat. "Then the drug took over. You collapsed and the thermos rolled aside."

"A drug—in the coffee."

"It fits. Whoever kidnapped you was nervous and under enormous pressure. They didn't take the time to look for the thermos. Why should they? They had you."

"Then it would have to be someone who knew my habits, who knew that I was coming here that day. Someone who…" She trailed off as she looked down at the thermos.

"Someone who's close to you," he finished. He lifted the thermos. "This close."

She felt the chill. The urge to look over her shoulder, to run came back in full force. Using all her self-control, she remained still. "What do we do now?"

"Now we find out who fixed your coffee and who might have had the opportunity to add something extra to it."

It wasn't easy to nod, but she did. "Reeve, shouldn't the police have gotten this far?"

He looked past her, into middle distance. "You'd think so, wouldn't you?"

She looked down at the rings on her hand—one a diamond that should have symbolized faith. One of sapphires that should have symbolized love. "My father," she began, but could go no further.

"It's time we talked to him."

It was dangerous for them to meet, but each drove down the long, rough road to the cottage. This was a time it would have been more dangerous not to meet.

The spot was isolated, overgrown, unlovely—a forgotten little cottage on a forgotten plot of land that had never been successfully tilled. That's why it had been perfect. It was close enough to the little farm to have been convenient, far enough away from town to go unnoticed.

The windows were boarded, except for one where the boards had been hacked away. They'd already discussed burning the place down, leaving the ashes to rot—like the body they'd buried in the woods behind.

The cars arrived within moments of each other. The two people were too disciplined, too cautious to be late. And both as they approached each other, were strung tight with nerves. Circumstances had made it necessary for them to trust the other with their lives.

"She's beginning to remember."

An oath, pungent and terrified. "You're sure?"

"I wouldn't have contacted you otherwise. I value my life as much as you value yours." They both knew as long as one remained safe, so did the other. And if one made a mistake...

"How much does she know?"

"Not enough to worry yet. Childhood memories, a few images. Nothing of this." A crow cawed frantically overhead, making both of them jolt. "But things are coming back. It's more than just nightmares now. I think if she pushes, really pushes, it's all going to come back."

"We've always known it would come back. All we need is a bit more time."

"Time?" The derisive laugh startled a squirrel. "We've precious little left. And she tells the American everything. They're lovers now—and he's clever. Very clever. I sometimes think he suspects."

"Don't be a fool." But nerves twisted and tightened. How could the American have been anticipated? "If that idiot Henri hadn't gotten drunk. *Merde!*" They'd seen their carefully executed plans shattered because of wine and lust. Neither of them regretted having to dig a grave.

"There's no use going over that now. Unless we can take her again the exchange is impossible. Deboque remains in prison, the money is out of reach and vengeance is lost."

"So we take her again. Who'd expect a second kidnapping to be attempted so soon?"

"We had her once!" It wasn't so much temper as fear. Both of them had lived on the edge since Brie had been identified at the hospital.

"And we'll have her again. Soon. Very soon."

"What about the American? He's not as trusting as the princess."

"Dispensable—as the princess will be if she remembers too much too soon. Watch her closely. You know what to do if it becomes necessary."

The small silenced gun with its lethal bullets was safely hidden. "If I kill her, her blood's on your hands, as well."

Thoughts of murder weren't troubling. Thoughts of

failure, of discovery were. "We both know that. Our luck only has to hold until the night of the ball."

"The plan's mad. Taking her there, right from the palace when it's filled with people."

"The plan can work. Have you a better one?" There was only silence for a moment, but it wasn't a comfortable one.

"I wish to God I'd stayed here with her, instead of that fool Henri."

"Just keep your eyes and ears open. You've gained her trust?"

"As much as anyone."

"Then use it. We've less than two weeks."

Chapter 10

Brie sat with her hands folded in her lap, her back very straight and her eyes level. She waited for her father to speak. Questions, too many of them, had formed in her mind. Answers, too many of them, had yet to be resolved.

Who was she? She'd been told—Her Serene Highness Gabriella de Cordina, daughter, sister. A member of the Bissets, one of the oldest royal families of Europe.

What was she? She'd learned—a responsible woman with an organized mind, a sense of duty and not so quiet wells of passion. But something had happened to take the rest away from her, those vital little details that make a person whole. She was only just beginning to fight for the right to have them back.

Drugged coffee, a dark room, voices. A knife and blood on her hands. She needed those memories, those details to have the rest. She'd just begun to face this.

The room was very quiet. Through the west windows, the light was lovely, serene. It turned the red carpet to blood without violence.

"So you believe the coffee Gabriella carried in this was drugged." Armand spoke without heat as he glanced at the red thermos that sat on his desk.

"It's logical." Reeve didn't sit. He faced Armand, as well, standing just beside Brie's chair. "It also fits in with the recurring dream Brie has."

"The thermos can be analyzed."

"Yes, and should be." Though his eyes were very calm, he watched Armand's every movement, every expression. Just as he knew Armand watched his. "The question is why it wasn't found before this."

Armand met Reeve's gaze. When he spoke, he spoke with authority, not with friendship. "It would appear the police have been careless."

"It would appear a great many people have been careless." It wasn't as easy as it had once been, Reeve discovered, to hold back temper. He saw nothing on Armand's face but cool, steady calculation. And he didn't like it. "If the coffee was drugged, as I believe it was, the implications are obvious."

Armand drew out one of his long, dark cigarettes and lit it slowly. "Indeed."

"You take it very calmly, Your Highness."

"I take it as I must."

"And I as I must. I'm taking Brie out of Cordina until this business is resolved. She isn't safe in the palace."

Armand's jaw tensed, but only briefly. "If I hadn't been concerned for her safety, I wouldn't have brought you here."

"Without the bond between our families, I never would have come." Reeve's reply was mild and final. "It's not enough anymore. Now I want answers."

Armand was suddenly and completely royal. "You have no right to demand them of me."

Reeve took one step forward. He needed only one. "Your crown won't protect you."

"Enough!" Brie sprang out of the chair to stand between Reeve and her father. If it was a protective move, it wasn't a conscious one. She couldn't have said which of the two she sought to protect. Her anger whipped through her with a force that helped smother other emotions. "How dare the two of you speak around me as if I were incapable of thinking for myself? How dare the two of you *protect* me as though I were incompetent?"

"Gabriella!" Armand was out of his chair before it

fully registered how often he'd heard and dealt with that tone before. "Mind your tongue."

"I won't." Infuriated, she turned on him, leaning over the desk with both palms pressed to it. Another time he would have thought her magnificent—as her mother had been. "I won't be polite and inoffensive. I'm not a cotton-candy princess to be displayed, but a woman. It's my life, do you understand? I won't stand here silently while the pair of you bully each other like a couple of arrogant children over the same prize. I want answers."

Armand's eyes were cool and remote. So was his voice. "You want more than I'm free to give."

"I want what's mine by right."

"What's yours is yours only when I give it to you."

Brie straightened, pale but steady. "Is this a father?" Her voice was soft yet cut like a knife. "You rule Cordina well, Your Highness. Can the same be said for your family?"

It struck clean to the bone. Not a muscle on his face moved. "You have to trust me, Gabriella."

"Trust?" Her voice wavered only once. "This," she told him with a gesture toward the thermos. "This shows me I can't trust anyone. Not anyone," she repeated. Turning, she fled from both of them.

"Let her go," Armand ordered when Reeve was halfway across the room. "She's looked after. I tell you she's looked after," he repeated when Reeve continued toward the door. "Let her go."

The words wouldn't have stopped him, but the tone did. There was pain in it, the same vibrant pain Reeve had heard in Armand's voice that day in the hospital waiting room. Because of it, he paused at the doorway and looked back.

"Don't you know her every movement is watched?" Armand said quietly. "So closely that I know where she spent last night." Weariness exposed, he sat.

Reeve stayed where he was, eyes narrowed. He hadn't missed how often servants busied themselves near Brie, but he'd thought it Alexander's doing. "You have her spied on?"

"I have her looked after," Armand said very slowly. "Do you think I'd leave her safety to chance, Reeve? Or even in your very capable hands alone? I needed you for all the reasons I've stated, but with my daughter's life I use everything available to me." Armand ran his hands over his face briefly, but the gesture was his first outward sign of tension. "Please, close the door and stay. It's time you know more than I've told you."

A man had to trust his instincts. He could live or die by them. Reeve shut the door quietly and came back to the desk. "What game are you playing, Armand?"

"One that will keep my country, my people at peace.

One that will, God willing, bring my child back, safe and whole. One that will bring those who wish it differently punished." He picked up the smooth white rock. "Well punished," he whispered as he squeezed his hand tight. He'd vowed it already to the wife he'd loved and lost.

"You know who took her." Reeve's voice was quiet, but the anger still vibrated beneath. "You've known all along."

"Know of one, suspect another." Armand's hand opened and closed on the rock. "You suspect, as well." His eyes, hard and cold, stayed on Reeve's. "I'm not unaware that you've looked into matters, studied the facts, have certain theories. I'd expected no less. However, I hadn't expected you to share your thoughts with Gabriella."

"Who had a better right?"

"I'm her father, but her ruler first. Her rights are mine to give, mine to take." The arrogance was there, the cold, hard power Reeve recognized, even admired.

"You've used her."

"And you," Armand agreed. "And others. The picture's too large, too complex to bring it down to the kidnapping of my daughter. Her Serene Highness Gabriella de Cordina was abducted. My actions are as a result."

"Why did you ask me here?"

"Because I could trust you, as I told you in the beginning. Because I was aware that you'd soon tire of sitting on the sidelines. You'd think, you'd assimilate, and eventually you'd act. I had no intention of allowing you to act until the time was right. It nearly is."

"Why in hell are you leaving her in the dark?" Reeve demanded. "Don't you know how she suffers?"

"You think I don't know how she suffers?" Armand's voice rose, his eyes flared. In his youth he'd been known and feared for his lethal temper. For a moment, the control of twenty years nearly slipped away. "She's my child. My first child. I held her hands as she learned to walk, sat by her bed when she was restless with fever, wept with her by her mother's grave."

Rigid, Armand rose to stride to the window. There he leaned out, his fingers digging into the wood of the sill. "What I do," he said more calmly, "I do because I must. I love her no less."

If he believed nothing else, Reeve believed that. "She needs to know it."

Pride and regret moved through the prince, but above all, was responsibility. "The mind is a delicate thing, Reeve, and we're still so ignorant of it. Gabriella, for all her strength, all her will, isn't able to overcome her mind's decision not to remember. If you thought differently, why haven't you told her what you suspect? Who you suspect?"

"She needs time," Reeve began, and Armand turned back to him.

"Yes. I can do nothing more than give it to her. I'm advised, strongly advised, by Dr. Kijinsky that if Gabriella is told everything before her mind is ready to hear it, understand it, accept it, the shock might cause a breakdown. Her mind might refuse ever to remember."

"She's begun to remember bits and pieces."

"A button's pushed and the mind reacts." Armand continued to move the white rock in his palm. "You've studied enough to know. But if I were to tell her everything I know or suspect, it might be too much, an avalanche. As a father, I have to wait. As ruler of Cordina, I have ways of learning or discovering what I need to know. Yes, I know who took her, and why." Something fierce came into his eyes. The hunter, or the hunted, would understand it. "But the time isn't right. To have them, I need time. As someone who worked closely with—shall we say, governmental intrigue in Washington—you understand. No need to deny," he went on before Reeve could form a response. "I'm well aware of the work you did."

"I was a cop."

"And more," Armand said with a nod. "But we'll leave it at that. You understand that as a ruler I must have absolute proof before I make an accusation. I can't show the weakness of a father in rage over his child; I must be a judge seeking justice. There are some close to me who believe that because of my position I'm not aware of the maneuvers, the bribes, the false loyalties that swim under the surface of my reign. I'm content that they stay unaware. There are some who might think because I have Gabriella back that I wouldn't look further into the motive for her kidnapping. One of the ransom demands was the release of several prisoners. All but one was camouflage. There was only one—Deboque."

The name struck a chord. It was a name Reeve had heard often in his less publicized work in law enforcement. Deboque was a businessman, a successful one who'd exported drugs, women, guns. He'd dealt in everything from controlled substances to explosives, selling to the highest bidder.

Or he'd been successful, Reeve amended, until a concentrated three-year investigation had unmasked and convicted him. It was widely believed that during the two years Deboque had served so far, he'd continued to pull the strings in his organization.

"So you think Deboque's behind it?"

"Deboque kidnapped Gabriella," Armand said simply. "We have only to prove through whom."

"And you know?" Reeve paused, at last thinking coolly. To accuse anyone close would cause an uproar. Only clear-cut proof would dim it. Only precise proof

could tie Deboque in and stop what maneuvers and po-
litical machinations he'd already begun. "Can Deboque
pull the strings of power in Cordina even from a cell?"

"He believes he's already begun. I think with this—"
Armand turned his hand toward the thermos "—it should
be a simple matter to twist his string and name one. The
other is more difficult." He looked down at his hands a
moment, at the ring only he could wear. Some emotion
ran quickly over his face. Reeve thought it was regret.
"I told you I know where Gabriella spent the night."

"Yes. With me."

Emotion flared again, and was just as quickly controlled. "You're the son of an old friend and a man I respect for himself, but it's difficult to be calm even though
I know she went to you. Intellectually, I accept that she's
a woman. However..." He trailed off. "Tell me your feelings for Gabriella. This time I ask as her father."

Still standing, Reeve looked down into Armand's face.
"I'm in love with her."

Armand felt the break, bittersweet, that a parent feels
when a child gives love and loyalty to another. "It's time
I told you what has been done. And time I asked for your
advice." Armand gestured to a chair and waited. There
were no more questions. This time Reeve sat.

They talked quietly, calmly for twenty minutes,
though each of them fought his own personal emotional

war. Once Armand went to a cabinet and poured two
snifters of brandy. The plan was solid. One more of the
reasons he'd maneuvered to have Reeve in Cordina was
to have the advantage of Reeve's mind, his experience.

The suspects were closely watched. The moment Brie
began to remember, the next move would be made. If all
went accordingly, Brie would never be in danger.

But things don't always go according to plan.

Brie swept into her office, temper bubbling, to find
Janet filing. Immediately, the papers still in her hand,
Janet turned and curtsied.

"Your Highness, I didn't expect you back today."

"I need to work." Going straight to her desk, she began
to flip through papers. "Do we have the personal menu
for the guests who attend the dinner before the ball?"

"The calligrapher sent one for your approval."

"Yes, here." Brie took out the heavy, cream-colored
paper and skimmed over the exquisite scroll. Each of the
seven courses was complemented by a different wine.
She'd selected each herself. Every dish that would be
served had been of her choosing. It was a meal even the
most rigid or fussy of gourmets would applaud. It wasn't
merely flawless, but a work of art, both on paper and in
reality. It made her temper boil over.

"I won't tolerate it." She slammed the menu down and sprang up to pace.

"The menu isn't suitable, Your Highness?"

"Not suitable?" With a laugh Brie dug her hands in her pockets. "It's perfection. Call the calligrapher and tell him to go ahead with them. The fifty who dine with us on the evening of the ball will have a dinner they won't forget. I've seen to that, haven't I?" Passion brimming in her eyes she whirled back. "I've arranged a lasting memory for a select few."

Unsure how to respond, Janet remained by the file with the papers still in her hand. "Yes, Your Highness."

"Yet even my father denies me the same courtesy."

"I'm sure you misunderstand," Janet began. "Prince Armand—"

"Has chosen to make decisions for me," Brie finished in a rush. "To play games, to conceal. I know that. I know that though there are hundreds of other things I don't know. But I will know." Brie curled her hands into fists. "And soon."

"You're upset." Janet set the papers aside, neat and orderly, to be dealt with later. "I'll order you some coffee."

"Wait." Brie took a step forward. "Who sees to my coffee, Janet?"

Thrown off by the demand in Brie's tone, Janet set the

phone down again. "Why, the kitchen, of course, Your Highness. I'll just ring down and—"

It ran through Brie's mind that she had no idea where the kitchens were. Had she ever? "Does the kitchen also prepare a thermos for me when I require one?" Her pulse had begun to beat too fast as she took the next step. "On an outing, Janet."

Janet made a flustered little gesture with her hands. "You prefer your coffee very strong. Habitually the old retainer brews it for you. The old Russian woman."

"Nanny," Brie murmured. It wasn't what she wanted to hear.

"I've often heard you joke that her coffee could stand firm without the thermos." Janet gave a little smile as if to lighten the mood. "She brews it in her room and refuses to give the cook the recipe."

"So she brings me the thermos before I go out."

"Traditionally, Your Highness. In the same way, Prince Bennett will take her, rather than his valet, a shirt if the button's loose."

Nausea came and was forced away. "A very old and trusted member of the family."

"She would consider herself more than staff, yes, Your Highness. The Princess Elizabeth would often take her rather than a personal maid when she traveled."

"Was Nanny with my mother in Paris? Was she with her when my mother become ill?"

"I've been told so, Your Highness. Her devotion toward Princess Elizabeth was complete."

And distorted? Brie wondered. Somehow twisted? How many people would have had the opportunity to doctor that thermos of coffee? Forcing herself to be calm, Brie asked the next question. "Do you know if Nanny brought me a thermos of coffee on the day I went to the little farm? The day I was abducted?"

"Why, yes." Janet hesitated. "She brought it to you here. You were taking care of a few letters before you left. She brought you the coffee, scolding you about taking a jacket. You laughed at her, promised her you wouldn't leave without one and hurried her along. You were impatient to begin, so you told me we'd see to the rest of the correspondence later. You took the thermos and left."

"No one came in?" Brie asked. "There were no interruptions from the time Nanny brought in the thermos to when I left with it?"

"No one came, Your Highness. Your car was waiting out front. I walked down with you myself. Your Highness…" Cautiously Janet held out a hand. "Can it be wise for you to dwell on such things, to pressure yourself with details like this?"

"Perhaps not." Brie accepted the hand briefly before she turned to the window. God, how she needed to talk, to talk to a woman. How she needed to trust. "I won't need you any more today, Janet. Thank you."

"Yes, Your Highness. Should I order your coffee before I go?"

"No." She nearly laughed. "No, I'm not in the mood for it."

But she couldn't stay inside, within the walls. Brie discovered that almost from the moment Janet left her. Thinking only that she wanted air and sun, Brie went out of her office. Though she hadn't realized she'd planned it, she found herself drawn to the terrace where she'd walked with Reeve that first night. Where he'd first kissed her. Where she'd first begun to test the feelings sleeping, not too quietly, inside her.

It was different during the day, she thought as she walked to the stone wall and leaned out. Different, but it wasn't any less lovely. She could see the mountains—stacks of rock, really—that sheltered Cordina from the rest of Europe. They had been a formidable defense in earlier centuries when foreign powers had lusted after the tiny country by the sea.

Then there was the sea itself, banked by sturdy stone walls. Here and there were cannons still at strategic points in the embankment, reminders of pirates and swift-sailing frigates and other threats from the sea.

Closer was the capital city itself, serene in its antiquity, content with its label of "quaint."

She loved it. Brie didn't need facts or details of the past to feel. Cordina was home and a refuge. It was past and future. Every day she lived there, she felt the need to be able to reach out and hold what was hers increase. Every day she lived there, her resentment at the block that prevented her from doing so grew.

"Your Highness." Loubet stepped onto the terrace, favoring his hip only slightly. "I hope I'm not disturbing you."

He was, but her manners were too ingrained. Brie smiled as she held out her hands. In any case, she had discovered over the dinner they'd shared that she liked Loubet's young, pretty wife very much. And she'd found it sweet that the stuffy, practical minister of state should be so obviously in love.

"You look well, Monsieur."

"Merci, Votre Altesse." He brought her hand up, giving it an avuncular brush of lips. "I must say, you're blooming. Being home is the best medicine, *oui*?"

"I was thinking—" she turned back to her view of Cordina "—that it feels like home. Not always inside, but out here. Have you come to see my father, Monsieur Loubet?"

"Yes, I have an appointment with him in a moment."

"Tell me, you've worked with my father for many years. Are you also his friend?"

"I've considered myself so, Your Highness."

Always so conservative, Brie thought with a flash of impatience. Always so diplomatic. "Come, Loubet, without the amnesia, this is certainly a question I wouldn't have to ask. And after all," she reminded him with a slow lift of brow, "it is on your advice that my problem remains a discreet one. So tell me, has my father friends, and are you one of them?"

He didn't hesitate, but paused. Loubet was a man who would always gather his thoughts together, sift through them meticulously, then put them into words. "There are few great men in the world, Your Highness. Some of these are good, as well. Prince Armand is one of these. Great men make enemies, good men draw friends. Your father has the burden of doing both."

"Yes." With a sigh, she rested against the wall. "I think I understand that."

"I'm not Cordinian." Loubet smiled as he looked out over the city with her. "By law, the minister of state is French. I love my own country. I can tell you frankly that I would not serve yours but for my feelings toward your father."

"I wish I were so sure of my feelings," she murmured.

"Your father loves you." He said it gently, so gently Brie had to close her eyes or weep. "Have no doubt there is nothing more important to Prince Armand than your welfare."

"You make me ashamed."

"Your Highness—"

"No, rightly so. I have a great deal to think about." Straightening from the wall, Brie held out her hand again. "Thank you, Loubet."

He bowed formally, making her smile. Then Brie forgot him as she turned back to the view and thought of her father.

Neither of them had paid any attention to the young man arranging pots of flowers farther down the terrace. Or the sturdy maid dusting glass just inside the doors.

Armand was keeping something from her. Of that she was certain. She knew nothing, however, of his reasons. Perhaps they were good ones. Yet even as she conceded this, the resentment didn't fade. Whatever her father or anyone else thought she should or shouldn't do, she'd have to find out.

Reeve found her there—after looking everywhere else he could think of. He had to control both his impatience and his relief as he stepped onto the terrace. Armand had assured him Brie was looked after—and he noticed the two people going about their business not too close to the princess, but close enough. But the prince had been cautious enough to enlist his help from the beginning, as well.

After their conversation, Reeve understood better why Armand had called in the help of an outsider, one whose feelings for Cordina and the royal family were more or less secondhand. Or had been, Reeve thought as he stood looking at Gabriella. Now more than ever he needed his objectivity. And now more than ever he found it all but impossible to find.

"Brie."

She turned slowly, as if she'd known he was there. Her hair was ruffled a bit by the wind, but her eyes were calm. "The first night we walked here I had questions. So many of them. Now, weeks later, too few of them have been answered." She looked down at the rings on her hands—conflicting emotions, conflicting loyalties. "You won't tell me what you spoke of with my father after I left."

It wasn't a question, but Reeve knew he had to answer it. "Your father thinks of you before he thinks of anything else, if that helps."

"And you?"

"I'm here for you." He came to her so that they stood as they had once before, under the moonlight. "There's no other reason."

"For me." She looked at him, searching, fighting not to let her heart lead her mind. "Or to satisfy an old family bond?"

"How much do you want?" he demanded. When he grabbed her hands he wasn't thinking of how small and delicate they were but of how strong, how searing her eyes could be. "My feelings for you have nothing to do with family bonds. And my being here now has everything to do with my feelings for you."

But what were they? she wondered. He seemed so careful not to tell her. Was it so difficult for him to say, "I care"? Brie looked down at their joined hands. Perhaps for him it was, she reflected. Not all fairy tales ended happily ever after. Reeve wasn't a knight galloping to sweep up the princess and carry her off. He was a man. She hadn't given her heart to a knight.

"I want this to be over," she said encapsulating everything from her blank past to the uncertain present. "I want to feel safe again."

The hell with objectivity, with plans. He took her by the shoulders. "I'll take you to America for a while."

Puzzled, she put a hand to his arm, holding on or holding off, she didn't know. "To America?"

"You can stay with me on the farm until this whole business is over."

Until. The word reminded her that some things had to end. Just end. She dropped her hand. "This whole business begins with me. I can't run from it."

"There's no need for you to stay here." Suddenly he saw how simple it could be. She'd be away. He could keep her safe. Armand would simply have to alter his plan.

"There's every need for me to stay. My life is lost here somewhere. How can I find it thousands of miles away?"

"When you're ready to remember, you'll remember. It won't matter where you are."

"It matters to me." She drew away from him then, backing up until she was braced against the wall. Pride came back, as much a part of her inheritance as the color of her eyes. "Do you think I'm a coward? Do you think I'd turn my back and walk away from the people who used me? Has my father asked you to do this so I won't ask any more questions?"

"You know better."

"I know nothing," she retorted. "Nothing except that all the men in my life seem compelled to shield me from what I don't want to be shielded from. This morning you said we'd work together."

"I meant it."

She watched him carefully. "And now?"

"I still mean it." But he didn't tell her what he knew. He didn't tell her what he felt.

"Then we will." But she didn't tell him what she'd learned. She didn't tell him what she needed.

She did step forward, even as he did. She did reach for him as he reached for her. They held each other close, both knowing that so much lay between them.

"I wish we were alone," she murmured. "Really alone, as we were the day on the boat."

"We'll go sailing tomorrow."

She shook her head before she pressed her face harder against him. "I can't. There'll be no time between now and the ball for anything. So many obligations, Reeve."

For both of us, he thought. "After the ball, then."

"After." She kept her eyes closed for only another moment. "Will you make me a promise? A foolish one."

He kissed one temple, then the other. "How foolish?"

"Always practical." Smiling, she tilted her head back. "When the blanks are gone and this is over, really over, will you spend the day with me on the water?"

"That doesn't seem so foolish."

"You say that now." She linked her hands around his neck. She'd hold him there, if only for a moment. "But promise."

"I promise."

With a sigh, she melted against him. "I'll hold you to your word," she warned.

When their mouths met, neither of them wanted to go beyond the moment to that last day alone on the water.

Chapter 11

"So I told Professor Sparks that a man would have to be made of stone to concentrate on Homer when there was a woman who looked like Lisa Barrow in the same classroom."

"Did he sympathize?" Brie asked Bennett absently as she watched the freshly cleaned chandelier being raised back in place.

"Are you kidding? He's got the heart of a prune." Grinning, he stuck his hands in his back pockets. "But I got a date with the divine Miss Barrow."

Brie laughed as she checked the long list of notes she had on a clipboard. "I could tell you that you aren't going to Oxford to thicken your little black book."

"But you won't." Easily he slung an arm over her

shoulders. "You never lecture. I got a look at the guest list. It was a pleasure to see that the luscious Lady Lawrence will make it."

That got her attention. Brie lowered the clipboard and scowled at him. "Bennett, Lady Alison Lawrence is nearly thirty and divorced."

He gave her his charming choirboy look that had wickedness just around the edges. "So?"

Brie shook her head. Had he been born precocious? she wondered. "Maybe I should lecture."

"Now leave that to Alex. He's so much better at it."

"So I've discovered," she murmured.

"Has he been giving you a hard time?"

She was frowning again as she watched the next chandelier begin its journey up. "Does he usually?"

"It's just his way." The loyalty was there, too strong to waver.

"Prince Perfect."

His face brightened. "Why, you remember—"

"Dr. Franco told me."

"Oh." His arm tightened briefly, both in reassurance and disappointment. "I didn't have much time to talk to you last night when I got in. I've wanted to ask you how you were."

"I wish I could tell you—along the windows, please," she directed as men brought in two twenty-foot tables.

They'll be covered with white linen, she thought as she checked her clipboard again, then laden with little delicacies to help the guests get through the long night of the ball. "Physically, I've been given the nod, with reluctance. I think Dr. Franco would like to pamper me a while longer. Everything else is complicated."

He took her hand, turning the diamond so that the facets caught the light. "I guess this is one of those complications."

She tensed, then relaxed. He could feel it. "Only temporarily. Things are bound to fall into place soon." She thought of the dreams, of the thermos. "Bennett, I've been wanting to ask you about Nanny. Do you think she's well?"

"Nanny?" He gave her a quick look of surprise. "Has she been ill? No one told me."

"No, not ill." Brie hesitated because the war of loyalties confused her. Why didn't she simply tell what she suspected about her old nurse? Tell and be done with it? "But she's quite old now, and people often become odd or…"

"Senile? Nanny?" This time he laughed as he squeezed her hand. "She's got a mind like a brick. If she's been fussing around you too much, it's only because she feels entitled."

"Of course." Her doubts didn't fade, but she kept them

to herself. She'd watch and wait, as she'd promised herself.

"Brie, there's a rumor running around that you and Reeve are the love match of the decade."

"Oh?" She only raised a brow, but her thumb came around to worry the diamond on her finger. "Apparently we're playing the game well."

"Is it—a game, I mean?"

"Not you, too?" Impatient, she walked away from him toward the terrace doors. "I've done this round with Alexander already."

"It's not a matter of pushing my exalted nose in." Equally impatient, he followed her. Though they were close to an argument, they kept their voices low. Servants were notorious for their excellent hearing. "It's only natural for me to be concerned."

"Would you be so concerned if the engagement were genuine?" Her voice was cool, too cool. That alone gave Bennett the answer to his question. But it didn't tell him whether he should be relieved or disturbed.

"I feel responsible," he said after a moment. "After all, it was more or less my idea, and—"

"Yours?" This time she set her clipboard down on a table with a snap.

Bennett fumbled a bit, wishing he'd kept his mouth shut and his eyes open. If there was one thing he avoided, it was an argument with a woman. He was bound to lose. "Well, I did point out to Father that it would look a little odd for Reeve to be escorting you everywhere, living here, and... Hell." Frustrated by her calm, icy look, he dragged a hand through his hair. "There had been all kinds of talk. *Commérage*."

"What do I care for gossip?"

"You've never had to deal with that kind before." His voice wasn't bitter, but resigned. "Look, Brie, I might be the youngest of the three of us, but I'm the one with the most experience with the tacky little tabloids."

"Justifiably, it would seem."

He, too, could become very dignified. "Yes, quite justifiably. But while I've chosen to live my life a certain way, you haven't. I couldn't stand seeing your name and picture splashed all over, sneered over. You can be angry if you like. I'd rather have you angry than hurt ever again."

She could have been furious with him. Brie understood it was her right to be. She could have told him, stiffly and finally, to stay out of her affairs. That by interfering, he'd made her more vulnerable than any scandal would. The ring on her hand was a prop—a support. One day she'd look down and it would be gone. It would be over.

She could have been angry, but love poured through

her, warm and sweet. He was so young, and so inherently kind. "Damn you, Bennett." But her arms went around him. "I should be furious with you."

He rested his cheek against her temple. "I couldn't know you'd fall in love with him."

She could deny it and save some pride. Instead she shook her head and sighed. "No, neither could I."

Just as Brie drew back, she saw a footman escort two women into the room. She'd left instructions that Christina Hamilton and her sister were to be brought to her as soon as they arrived.

From the photos and newspaper clippings she'd been given, Brie recognized the tall, striking brunette in the Saint Laurent suit. She felt nothing but a moment's blank panic.

What should she do? She could rush across the room or smile and wait. Should she be polite or warm, affectionate or amused? God, how she hated not simply knowing.

"She's your closest friend," Bennett murmured in his sister's ear. "You've said you had brothers by birth but a sister by luck. That's Christina."

It was enough to ease the panic. Both women had begun their curtsies, the younger with an eye on the prince, the older with a grin for Brie. Falling back on instinct, Brie crossed the room, both hands outstretched. Christina met her halfway.

"Oh, Brie." Laughing, Christina held her at arm's length. Brie saw that her eyes were soft, but full of irony. The mouth was lovely in a smile, but it was strong. "You look wonderful, wonderful, wonderful!" Then Brie was caught in a hard hug. Christina smelled expensive and feminine and unfamiliar. But the panic didn't return.

"I'm glad you're here." Brie let her cheek rest against Christina's expertly swept-back hair. It wasn't a lie, she discovered. She needed a friend—simply a friend, not family, not a lover. "You must be exhausted."

"Oh, you know flying leaves me wired for hours. You've lost weight. How unkind of you."

Brie was smiling when she drew away. "Only five pounds."

"Only five." Christina rolled her eyes. "I'll have to tell you the horrors of that pricey little spa I went to a few months ago. I gained five. Prince Bennett." Christina held out her hand, casually expecting it to be kissed. "Good God, is it the air in Cordina that makes everyone look so spectacular?"

Bennett didn't disappoint her. But as his lips brushed her knuckles, his gaze shifted to Eve. "The air in Houston must be magic."

Christina hadn't missed the look. Like the kiss,

she'd expected it. After all, Eve wasn't a young woman any man could ignore. That's what worried Christina. "Prince Bennett, I don't believe you've met my sister, Eve."

Bennett already had Eve's hand. His lips lingered over it only seconds longer than they had over her sister's. But a few seconds can be a long time. He noted the long fall of rich, dark hair, the dreamy, poetic blue eyes, the wide, full curve of her mouth. His young heart was easily lost.

"I'm happy to meet you, Your Highness."

Her voice wasn't that of a girl, but of a woman, as rich and dark as her hair.

"You look lovely, Eve." Brie took Eve's hands herself to ward off her brother. "I'm so glad you could come."

"It's just the way you described it." Eve sent her a sudden, alarmingly effective smile—alarming because it was as natural as a sunrise. "I haven't been able to look fast enough."

"Then you should take your time." Smoothly Bennett brushed his sister aside. "I'll give you a tour. I'm sure Brie and Chris have lots to talk about." With a half bow to the other women, he led Eve from the room. "What would you like to see first?"

"Well." Not certain if she should frown or laugh, Brie looked after them. "He certainly moves fast."

"Eve doesn't creep along herself." Christina tapped

her foot a moment, then dismissed them. After all, she couldn't play chaperon forever. "How busy are you?"

"Not very," Brie told her, mentally rearranging her schedule. "Tomorrow I won't have time to take a breath."

"Then let's take one now." Christina linked an arm through hers. "Can we have tea and cookies in your rooms, the way we used to? I can't believe it's been a year. There's so much to catch up on."

If you only knew, Brie mused as she moved down the corridor with her.

"Tell me about Reeve," Christina demanded as she plucked an iced pink cookie from the tray.

Brie ran her spoon around and around in her tea, though she'd forgotten to put any sugar in. "I don't know what to tell you."

"Everything," Christina said dramatically. "I'm eaten up with curiosity." She'd tossed off her shoes and had her legs curled under her. The excitement of the flight was beginning to ease into relaxation. But she'd already noticed that Brie wasn't relaxed. She dismissed it—al-most—as tension over the ball. "You certainly don't have to tell me what he looks like." She gestured with the half cookie, then nimbly popped it into her mouth. "I see his picture every time I pick up a magazine. Is he fun?"

Brie thought about the day on her boat, about the

drives they sometimes took along the coast. She thought of the dinner parties they attended when he would murmur something in her ear that was rude and accurate. "Yes." It made her smile. "Yes, he's fun. And he's strong. He's clever and rather arrogant."

"You've got it bad," Christina murmured, watching her friend's face. "I'm happy for you."

Brie tried to smile, but couldn't quite pull it off. Instead she lifted her cup. "You'll meet him soon and be able to judge for yourself."

"Hmmm." Christina studied the tray of elegant cookies, lectured herself, then chose one, anyway. "That's one of the things that's bothered me."

Instantly alert, Brie set down her tea again. "Bothered you?"

"Well, yes, Brie. Where *did* you meet him? I can't believe you met this wonderful, clever, arrogant man last year when you were in the States, then stayed with me for three days in Houston without breathing a word."

"Royalty's trained to be discreet," Brie said offhandedly, and pretended an interest in the cookies herself.

"Not that discreet," Christina said over a full mouth. "In fact, I remember you telling me specifically that there wasn't anyone in your life, that you weren't interested in men particularly. And I agreed heartily, because I'd just ended a disastrous affair."

Brie felt herself getting in deeper. "I suppose I wasn't entirely sure of my feelings—or his."

"How did you work it out long distance?"

"There's a connection through our fathers, you know." She dug back to something Reeve had said to her once, something she'd nearly forgotten. "Actually, we met years ago, here in Cordina. It was my sixteenth birthday party."

"You're not going to tell me you fell for him then?"

Brie merely moved her shoulders. How could she confirm or deny what she didn't know?

"Well." Christina poured more tea in her cup. Because she found the idea so sweet, she forgot about details. "That certainly explains why you didn't have much interest in all those gorgeous men in Paris. I'm happy for you."

She laid her hand over Brie's lightly, briefly. It was a very simple, very casual touch of friendship. Brie's eyes filled so that she had to fight to clear them.

"I'm glad he was here for you after…" Christina trailed off, no longer interested in her tea. When she set her legs down, she touched Brie's hand again, but the touch was firmer. "Brie, I wish you'd talk to me about it. The press is so vague. I know they haven't caught the people responsible, and I can't stand it."

"The police are investigating."

"But they haven't caught anyone. Can you rest easily until they do? I can't."

"No." Unable to sit, Brie rose, linking her hands. "No, I can't. I've tried to go on with the daily business of life, but it's like waiting, just waiting without knowing."

"Oh, Brie." Chris was at her side, hugging her. "I don't mean to pressure you, but we've always shared everything. I was so frightened for you." A tear brimmed over, but she brushed at it impatiently. "Damn, I told myself I wouldn't do this, but I can't help it. Every time I think about what it was like to pick up the paper and see the headline—"

Brie took a step back from the emotion. "You shouldn't think about it. It's over."

The tears cleared, but now there was puzzlement. "I'm sorry." Hurt, but unsure why, Christina looked down for her bag. "It's too easy to forget sometimes who you are and what rules you have to live by."

"No." Torn between instinct and a promise, Brie hesitated. "Don't go, Chris. I need—oh, God, I do need to talk to someone." Brie looked at her then and chose. "We're very good friends, aren't we?"

Puzzlement and hurt became confusion. "Brie, you know—"

"No, just tell me."

Christina set her bag back down again. "Eve's my sis-

ter," she said calmly. "And I love her. There's nothing in
the world I wouldn't do for her. I don't love you any less."

Brie closed her eyes a moment. "Sit down, please."
She waited, then sat down beside Christina. Taking one
long breath, she told her friend everything.

Perhaps Christina paled a bit, perhaps her eyes widened, but she interrupted Brie only twice to clarify.
When the story was finished, she sat in absolute silence for a moment. But, then, volcanoes often sit quietly.

"It stinks."

She said the words in her soft Texas drawl so that Brie
blinked. "I beg your pardon?"

"It stinks," Christina repeated. "Politics usually does,
and Americans are the first to say so, but this really
stinks."

For some reason, Christina's sturdy, inelegant opinion made her comfortable. Brie smiled and reached for
a cookie without thinking. "I can't really blame politics.
After all, I agreed to everything."

"Well, what else were you going to do, for heaven's
sake?" Exasperated, Christina rose and walked over to a
small cherry wood commode. She discovered she wanted
badly to break something. Anything. "You were weak,
disoriented and frightened."

"Yes," Brie murmured. "Yes, I was." She watched

Christina rummage and locate an exquisite little decanter.

"I need a brandy." Without ceremony, Christina poured. "You?"

"Mmmm." Brie only nodded an assent. "I didn't even know that was there."

Christina spilled a bit of brandy over the side of a glass, swore and blotted the drop with a finger. "You'll remember." She walked back, and her eyes were bright and strong when she handed Brie a snifter. "You'll remember because you're too stubborn not to."

And for the first time Brie believed it, completely. With something like relief she touched her glass to Christina's. "Thanks."

"If I hadn't let myself get talked out of it, I would have been here weeks ago." With an unintelligible mutter, Christina sat on the arm of the sofa. "Your father, that Loubet and the wonderful Reeve MacGee should all be rounded up, corralled and horsewhipped. I'd like to give all three of them a piece of my mind."

Brie laughed into her brandy. This was what she'd needed, she realized, to counterbalance that fierce protection from the men who cared for her. "I think you could do it."

"Damn right I could. I'm surprised you haven't."

"Actually, I have."

"That's more like it."

"The trouble is, my father does what he thinks best for me and the country. Loubet does what he thinks best for the country. I can't fault either of them."

"And Reeve?"

"And Reeve." Brie looked up from her glass. "I'm in love with him."

"Oh." Christina drew the word out as she studied Brie's face. She'd already made up her mind that she'd stay right there in Cordina until everything was resolved. Now she reaffirmed it. "So that part of it is real."

"No." She didn't let herself look down at her ring. "Only my feelings are real. The rest is just as I told you."

"Ah, well, that's no problem."

Though she didn't want pity, she had been expecting a bit of sympathy. "It's not?"

"Of course not. If you want him, you'll get him."

Both amusement and interest flickered over her face. "Will I? How?"

Christina took a quick swallow of brandy. "If you don't remember all the men you had to brush out from around your feet, I'm not going to tell you. It isn't good for my ego. Anyway, they're not worth it." She touched her glass to Brie's.

"Who isn't?"

"Men." Christina crossed her stockinged feet and examined her toes. "Men aren't worth it. Louses, every single one."

Somehow Brie felt they'd had this conversation before. A laugh bubbled in her throat. "Every one?"

"Every single one, bless 'em."

"Chris." This time Brie reached out. "I'm glad you came."

Chris leaned over and brushed her cheek. "Me, too. Now why don't you come to my room and help me pick out something devastating for dinner tonight?"

When Reeve came to her rooms, she wasn't there. He saw the depleted tray of cookies, the cooling tea. And the empty brandy snifters. Interesting, he thought. He knew Brie drank little, and almost never during the day. He thought she had either been relaxed or upset.

He'd been told Brie was entertaining Christina Hamilton, of the Houston Hamiltons. Rocking back on his heels, he studied the remains of the little tea party. He'd done some careful research on Brie's old college friend. They had passed the point where he'd take any chances. A call to a friend in D.C. who owed him a favor, and Reeve had everything from Christina Hamilton's birthday to her bank balance. He'd turned up nothing that shouldn't have been there. Yet he felt uneasy.

Not uneasy, he admitted as he wandered around Brie's

sitting room. Jealous. Jealous because she was spending time with someone else. It was laughable. He hated to think himself so tied to a woman that they couldn't spend an afternoon apart. He hated to think himself that unreasonable—or that sunk.

It was her safety, Reeve reminded himself. His feelings for her were tangled in concern. It was natural—but it wasn't comfortable. When there wasn't any more reason for concern, perhaps his feelings could change. It was logical. It would probably be for the best. It was, he thought ruefully, extremely unlikely.

He could smell her even now, though the room was delicate with the scent of the flowers that were always in vases here and there. It was here, that very feminine, very sexy, very French fragrance that habitually clung to her. He could picture her sitting on the love seat, sipping a cup of tea, nibbling at a cookie, perhaps, but without any real interest. She ate too little.

There had been strain. He knew it—hated it. She would feel dishonest talking with her old friend who was a stranger now.

Is that why he felt so strongly? he wondered. He was, of all the people in her life, the only one who had no strong ties from the past she couldn't remember. There weren't years of memories between them, drawing them together, pulling them apart. There was only now.

And that one night years before when he'd waltzed with her in the moonlight.

Idiot. He dragged a hand through his hair. He was an idiot to think that even without the amnesia she would have remembered a few dances with a man on her sixteenth birthday. Just because he'd never forgotten. Had never been able to forget. Had he been in love with her all this time? With the image of her?

Reeve picked up an earring she'd taken off and set carelessly on a table. It was an elegant design of gold and diamonds. Complex and simple, it changed as he turned it—like a woman. Like the woman. He twisted it in his fingers for a moment and wondered if it was still the image that captivated him.

He knew too much about her, he thought. Too many details that he had no business knowing. She liked her bathwater too hot, collected old pictures of people she didn't know. She'd once had a secret dream to dance with the Ballet Royal. When she'd been fifteen, she'd wondered if she was in love with a young gardener.

He knew before she did those foolish little details of her life. He'd stolen them from her, out of diaries he'd read to do a job. When she remembered all, when she looked at him then, how much would she resent the intrusion?

He knew now the two people who'd kidnapped her,

changed her life, stolen her past. He knew who they were and why they'd done so. For her sake, he couldn't tell her yet. He could only watch and protect. And when she knew all, when she looked at him then, how much would she resent the deception?

How could he tell her that two people close to her, two people she trusted, had plotted against her? Used her? It might ease his conscience, but what would it do to Brie?

He'd gone past the point where he'd taken any chances.

He heard the door to the bedroom open and paused with the earring still in his hand.

"Yes, thank you, Bernadette. If you'll just run the bath. I'll see to my own hair. We're dining *en famille* tonight."

"Yes, Your Highness."

He heard the maid move quietly into the bath, then the water striking porcelain. He imagined Brie undressing. Slowly. Unbuttoning the tailored little blouse he'd seen her put on that morning. Odd, he realized. He'd seen her dress in the mornings they'd woken together. But he'd never seen her undress. When he came to her she was already in a robe or nightgown. Or waiting naked in the bed.

Suddenly driven, he set down the earring and crossed into the bedroom.

She was standing in front of the mirror, but she hadn't

removed her clothes. There was a small porcelain box on her dresser with the lid off. She took pins from it, one by one, and swept up her hair.

She was thinking, but not, he realized, about what she was doing. Her eyes weren't focused on the reflection. But she was smiling, just a little, as if she were content. It wasn't often she smiled like that.

The maid came out to take a robe out of the closet. If she noticed Reeve in the sitting-room doorway, she gave no sign. As she laid the robe on the bed, Brie fastened the last pin.

"Thank you, Bernadette. I won't need you any more tonight. Tomorrow," she went on with a quick grin, "I'll exhaust you."

The maid curtsied. Reeve waited. The maid shut the door quietly behind her. Still, he waited. Brie put the top back on the box, running her finger over the porcelain when it was in place. With a little sigh, she stepped out of her shoes and stretched, eyes closed. Turning away from the mirror, she went to a small cabinet and switched on the CD player concealed inside. The music that came out was quiet, sultry. Something heard through open windows on summer nights. She unhooked her trim gray trousers, let them fall to the floor, then stepped out of them. While Reeve watched, she bent to pick them up, ran a hand down to smooth them and set them on the bed.

One by one, her mind on the music, she undid the buttons on her blouse. Beneath it she wore pearl-gray silk without frills. The teddy was as smooth as her skin, and very thin. She brushed the first slender strap from her shoulder before Reeve stepped forward.

"Gabriella."

She would have jumped or gasped if she hadn't recognized his voice. She turned slowly because she recognized the need in it, as well. He was standing just inside the room, but she could feel his heat and it immediately aroused her. He made no move, only watched, but she felt his touch slide over every inch of her. The sun was still strong enough to light the room, but her thoughts turned to night. And excitement.

Without a word she held out a hand.

Without a word he went to her.

They spoke with touches, the brush of a fingertip, the press of a palm. *You're mine. I've waited for you. I've ached for you.* Mouth moved over mouth silently, but hundreds of things were said. *This is all I've wanted. You're all I've needed. You.*

She undressed him, not too quickly. Each could feel the ache build to pain. It was exquisite. She drew his shirt from his shoulders, and still the only word that had been spoken between them was her name. In wordless agreement, they lowered themselves onto the bed.

He hadn't known any woman could make him want so badly. He had only to think of her to need. But to touch her...to feel her, soft and strong against him, was enough to make him forget he'd had a life before Gabriella.

He ran his hand over the silk, feeling it warm with the friction, feeling her move beneath. Her skin and the silk slid along his own flesh. Temptation. Her hands roamed over him freely, seeking pleasure, giving it. Desire. A kiss went on endlessly until they both were surrounded by every soft, every sweet sensation. Surrender.

Bric went limp, weakened by a deluge of feeling too strong to measure. He could do no more than go where the kiss led him. Into her.

The silk was brushed away with a stroke of his hand. When he slid inside her, the passion was subtle, timeless. Her breath shuddered. His muscles bunched, then flowed, then bunched again. Together they moved. Neither led, neither followed, because both were lost.

Her hands were firm on his shoulders; his fingers were curled into her hair. Their gazes locked as the rhythm matched the sultry heated music that dripped into the room.

It wasn't a matter of control, his or hers, but of mood. Savor. Prolong. He couldn't have described the sensations that rippled through him, overtook him, enclosed him, but he could have spoken in minute detail of what the sun did to her hair, of how pleasure affected her eyes.

She'd remember this always. If everything else was stripped from her again, Brie knew that this moment would remain perfectly clear.

There was no flash, no sudden storm of speed and desperation. They rose together, sweetly, gently, exquisitely. She could have wept from the beauty of it, but only smiled as his mouth touched hers.

They lay together comfortably, stretching out the moment a bit longer. The early-evening sunlight was quiet. If it hadn't been for obligations, they'd have stayed just so until the morning.

"I missed you."

Surprised, Brie tilted her head on his shoulder so that she could see his profile. "Did you?"

"I've hardly seen you today." He didn't feel as foolish saying it as he had felt thinking it. Smiling a little, he stroked her hair.

"I thought you might come up to the ballroom."

"I came by a couple of times. You were busy." And safe, he added to himself. Three of the workmen had carried guns under their vests.

"Tomorrow will be worse." Content, she snuggled against him. "It'll take hours to set up the flowers alone.

Then there's the wine and liquor, the musicians, the food. The people."

She fell silent. Unconsciously he drew her closer. "Nervous."

"A little. There will be so many faces, so many names. I wonder…"

"What?"

"I know just how important this ball is for the AHC and for Cordina. But I wonder if I can pull it off."

"You've done more than anyone can expect already." And he resented it. "Just relax and take it as it comes. Do what feels right for you, Brie."

She didn't speak for a moment, then plunged. "I have already." She shifted so that she could look at him directly. "I told Christina Hamilton everything."

He started to speak, then stopped himself. She was waiting, he could see, for criticism, impatience, even anger. He saw both the apology and the defiance in her eyes. "Why?" But it was a question, not an accusation. He could almost feel the relief from her.

"I couldn't lie to her. Maybe I couldn't remember, but I felt. I really felt something with her, something I needed." She paused only to make a sound of exasperation. "You'll think I'm foolish."

She started to sit up, so he went with her. "No." To

emphasize support, he laid a hand over hers. "Tell me what you felt."

"I needed to talk to a woman." She let out a long breath, then looked back at him. Her hair was tumbled, a sensuous mass over creamy shoulders. Her face still held the glow of passion. Yet vulnerability was there. "There are so many men in my life. Kind, concerned, but…" How could she phrase it so he'd understand? She couldn't. "I just needed to talk to a woman."

Of course she did. Reeve brought her hand to his lips. Why hadn't any of them seen it? Father, brother, doctor…lover. But she'd had no one to give her the kind of support, the kind of empathy only those of the same sex can give one another. "Did it help?"

She closed her eyes a moment. "Yes. Chris is special to me—that's what I felt."

"What was her reaction?"

"She said that it stinks." A giggle bubbled in her throat. A sound he'd heard too rarely. "She's of the opinion that you, my father and Loubet should be horsewhipped."

Reeve made a sound that might have been amusement or regret. Basically, it was agreement. "Sounds like a sensible woman."

"She is. I can't tell you what it meant just to talk to

her. Reeve, she didn't look at me as though I were ill or odd or…I don't know."

"Is that what we do?"

"Sometimes, yes." She brushed her hair back, looking at him with an eagerness that asked for understanding. "Chris took it all in, stated her opinion, then asked me to help her pick out a dress. It was all so natural, so easy, as if there weren't all these blanks between us. We were simply friends again, or still. I don't know how to explain it."

"You don't have to. But I'll have to talk to her."

Brie's lips curved. "Oh, I think she's planning on it." She kissed him then in the light, friendly manner she could assume so unexpectedly. "Thank you."

"For what?"

"For not telling me all the reasons I shouldn't have done it."

"The decision was always yours, Brie."

"Was it?" She laughed, shaking her head. "I wonder. My bath is cooling," she said, deliberately changing the mood. "You've detained me."

"So I have." Smiling, he ran a fingertip lightly down her breast and felt it tremble.

"The least you can do is wash my back."

"Sounds fair. Trouble is, I've missed my bath, as well."

"That shouldn't be a problem." She drew away from

him to rise. "I once wondered if I'd shared the tub with anyone. It's very large." Naked, with the sun filtering in behind her, she began to refasten her pins. "And we have more than an hour before dinner."

Chapter 12

Glitter. Glamour. Fantasy. That was a royal ball in a centuries-old palace. Elegance, sumptuousness, sophistication were what was expected when you brought together the rich, the famous and the royal.

Five Baccarat chandeliers trembled with light. Some of the colors couldn't even be named. A half-acre of floor gleamed, the color of aged honey. There was silver, crystal, white linen and masses and masses of flowers. But even these paled when compared to the glow of silks, the fire of jewels: the beautiful people.

Brie greeted the guests and tried to forget she was tired. For twelve hours she'd worked nonstop to make certain everything was perfect. It was. She had the satisfaction of that to offset her nerves. Cinderella had had her ball, she mused. But Cinderella hadn't had to deal with the florist.

There were gorgeous clothes and luxurious scents, but for her, there was a sea of faces and a mental list of names too long for comfort.

Her father was by her side, dressed in his most formal uniform. It reminded people that he'd been a soldier, a good one. But Brie thought he looked like a god—handsome, powerful. Remote.

She was curtsied to. Her hand was kissed. The conversations, thankfully, were brief and general before each person passed on to Reeve and her brothers.

She'd seen to the details, Brie reminded herself. Successfully. She'd succeed here, as well. She smiled at the man in the black silk jacket with the mane of white hair, recognizing him as one of the great actors of the century, one the British Queen had seen fit to knight. He took her hand, but kissed her cheek. Brie had been told he'd bounced her on his knee when she was a baby.

She was terrified, Reeve thought. And so beautiful. There was nothing he could do but be there. Protect, support—no matter how much she'd resent both. Had anyone told her she'd already pulled off a minor miracle? he wondered. She'd regained her strength, held on to her hope and given herself to her obligations.

Princess or not, she was a hell of a woman. For now, she was his.

She looked like a fairy tale tonight. Like the fairy tale he remembered from years before. There were diamonds in her hair, winking fire against fire. She wore them at her ears, subtle and effective, and at her throat in three dripping tiers. And on her hand, he reminded himself, as a symbol.

But while the fire danced around her, she'd chosen ice for her dress. A contrast in fashion? he wondered, or a statement that she had both?

White—stunning, cool, untouchable white—draped her. Slashing low at her throat to frame the fire there, rippling down her arms to meet the light and power on her fingers. Yards and yards of rich, smooth silk flowed down her until it nearly brushed the floor. Aloof, regal? So she was and so she looked. But the fire breathed around her passionately.

Once a man had had such a woman, would he ever, could he ever, turn to another?

"Did you see her?" Bennett mumbled so only Reeve could hear.

He'd only seen one woman, but he knew Bennett. "Who?"

"Eve Hamilton." Bennett gave a low sound of approval. "Just fantastic."

Beside him Alexander scanned the crowd and found her, but there wasn't any approval. She wore a ripe red dress that was cut beautifully, even conservatively. The color said one thing, the style another. "She's a child," he muttered. And he'd found her too precocious and too intelligent a child.

"You need glasses," Bennett told him, then smiled and kissed the hand of a dowager. "Or vitamins."

The line of guests seemed endless. Brie stood it by reminding herself just what the ball would mean to her charity. But when the last black tie and shimmering dress passed her, she almost sighed with relief.

It wasn't over, but with music there was some escape.

The orchestra knew its business. It took only a nod from her for the first waltz to begin. She held out her hand to Reeve. He'd open the ball with her this first and this last time. She let his arms and the music carry her. Sooner or later midnight would strike, and the dream would be over.

"You're beautiful."

They swirled together under the lights. "My dressmaker's a genius."

He did something they both knew was not quite acceptable. He kissed her. "That's not what I meant."

Brie smiled and forgot she was weary.

Prince Armand led out the sister of an exiled king.

Alexander chose a distant cousin from England. Bennett swept Eve Hamilton onto the floor. And so the ball began.

It was, as it should be, magical. Caviar, French wine, violins. Oil barons rubbing elbows with lords. Ladies exchanging gossip with celebrities. Brie knew it was her responsibility to be available to dance and to entertain; but it was a relief to discover she could enjoy it.

While she danced with Dr. Franco, she looked up at him and laughed. "You're trying to take my pulse."

"Nonsense," he told her, though he had been. "I don't have to be a doctor to look at you and know you're more than well."

"I'm beginning to believe I'll be completely well very soon."

His fingers tightened only slightly. "Has there been more?"

"These aren't your office hours," she told him with a smile. "And it's nothing you'd find with your little black bag. I simply feel it."

"Then the wait will have been worthwhile."

Her smile only faltered a little. "I hope so."

"Brie looks relaxed," Christina commented as she kept her hand light on Reeve's shoulder through the dance.

"Your being here helps."

She shot him a look. Though she'd seen to it that

they'd already had a private talk, Reeve hadn't completely mollified her. "It would have helped if I'd been here sooner."

He liked her, perhaps because of the tongue-lashing she'd delivered. "You still think I should be horse-whipped."

"I'm thinking it over."

"I want what's best for her."

She studied him a moment. "You're a fool if you don't already know what that is."

Brie worked her way expertly through the couples and the groups. Janet Smithers stood discreetly in a corner with her one and only glass of wine.

"Janet." Brie waved the curtsy aside. "I was afraid you'd decided not to come."

"I was late, Your Highness. There was some work I wanted to see to."

"No work tonight." Even as Brie took her hand she was casting around for a suitable dance partner for her secretary. "You look lovely," she added. Janet's dress was both plain and quiet, but it gave her a certain dignity.

"Your Highness." Loubet stepped to her side and bowed. "Miss Smithers."

"Monsieur." Brie smiled, thinking he'd be her solution.

"The ball is a wonderful success, as always."

"Thank you. It's going well. Your wife looks stunning."

"Yes." The smile bespoke pleasure and pride. "But she's deserted me. I'd hope Your Highness would take pity and dance with me."

"Of course." Brie sipped her wine, then found, to her satisfaction, that Alexander was within arm's reach. "But I've promised this dance to my brother." Plucking at his sleeve, she gave him a bland look before she turned back to her secretary. "I'm sure Miss Smithers would love to dance with you, wouldn't you, Janet?"

She'd successfully maneuvered them all. Pleased that she'd given her secretary a nudge onto the dance floor, Brie accepted Alexander's hand.

"That wasn't very subtle," he pointed out.

"But it worked. I don't want to see her huddling in a corner all night. Now someone else is bound to ask her to dance."

He lifted a brow. "Meaning me?"

"If necessary." She smiled up at him. "Duty first."

Alexander cast a look over Brie's shoulder. Loubet's slight limp was less noticeable in a dance. "She doesn't look thrilled to be dancing with Loubet. Maybe she has some taste, after all."

"Alex." But she laughed. "In any case, I haven't told you how handsome you look. You and Bennett—where is Bennett?"

"Monopolizing the little American girl."

"Little—oh, you mean Eve." She lifted a brow, noting the disapproval. "She's not that little. In fact, I believe she's just Bennett's age."

"He should know better than to flirt with her so outrageously."

"From what I've seen, it's hardly one-sided."

He made a restless move with his shoulders. "Her sister should keep a tighter rein on her."

"Alex." Brie rolled her eyes.

"All right, all right." But he skimmed the room until he'd found the slim brunette in the ripe red dress. And he watched her.

She lost track of how many dances she danced, how many glasses of wine she'd sipped at, how many stories and jokes she'd listened to. It had been, she realized, foolish to be nervous. It was all a blur, as such things should be. She enjoyed it.

She enjoyed it more when she found herself waltzing in Reeve's arms again.

"Too many people," he murmured against her ear. Slowly, skillfully, he circled with her toward the terrace doors. Then they were dancing in the moonlight.

"This is lovely." There were flowers here, too, creamy white ones that sent out a delicate vanilla fragrance. She could breathe it in without having it mixed with perfumes or colognes. "Just lovely."

"A princess should always dance under the stars."

She started to laugh as she looked up at him, but something rushed through her. His face seemed to change—recede, blur? She wasn't sure. Was it younger? Were the eyes more candid, less guarded? The scent of the flowers seemed to change. Roses, hot, humid roses.

The world went gray. For a moment there was no music, no fragrance, no light. Then he had her firmly by the arms.

"Brie." He would have swept her up, carried her to a chair, but she held him off.

"No, I'm all right. Just dizzy for a moment. It was…" She trailed off, staring up into his face as if she were seeing it for the first time. "We were here," she whispered. "You and I, right here, on my birthday. We waltzed on the terrace and there were roses in pots lining the wall. It was hot and close. After the dance you kissed me."

And I fell in love with you. But she didn't say it, only stared. She'd fallen in love with him when she was sixteen. Now, so many years later, nothing had changed. Everything had changed.

"You remember." She was trembling, so he held her lightly.

"Yes." Her voice was so quiet he leaned closer to hear. "I remember it. I remember you."

He knew better than to push, so he spoke gently. "Anything else? Do you remember anything else, or only that one night?"

She shook her head and would have drawn away. It hurt, she discovered. Memory hurt. "I can't think. I need—Reeve, I need a few moments. A few moments alone."

"All right." He looked back toward the ballroom, crowded with people. She'd never be able to make it through them now. Thinking quickly, he took her down the terrace, through another set of doors. "I'll get you to your room."

"No, my office is closer." She hung on, pushing herself to take each step. "I just want a moment to sit and think. No one will bother me there."

He took her because it was closer, and it would take him less time to go back for the doctor. It would take him less time to tell Armand that her memory was coming back and the next step had to be taken. The arrests would be made quietly.

The backup guard was well trained, Reeve told himself. He wouldn't have even known he was there if Armand hadn't explained that Brie was watched always, not only by Reeve, but by others.

The office was dark, but when he started to turn on the lights, she stopped him.

"No, please. I don't want the light."

"Come on, I'll sit with you."

Again she resisted. "Reeve, I need to be alone."

It was a struggle not to feel rejected. "All right, but I'm going to get the doctor, Gabriella."

"If you must." Her nails were digging into her palms as she fought for control. "But give me a few moments first."

If her voice hadn't warned him away, he would have held her. "Stay here until I get back. Rest."

She waited until he closed the door. Then she lay down on the little sofa in the corner of the room, not because she was tired, but because she didn't think she had even the strength to sit.

So many emotions. So many memories fighting to get through, and all at once. She'd thought that remembering would be a relief, as if someone released strings around her head that had been tied too tightly. But it hurt, it drained and it frightened.

She could remember her mother now, the funeral. The waves and waves and waves of grief. Devastation—hers, her father's, and how they'd clung to each other. She could remember a Christmas when Bennett had given her a silly pair of slippers with long elephant tusks curling out of them. She could remember fencing with Alexander and fuming when he'd disarmed her.

And her father, holding out his arms for her when she'd curled into his lap to pour out her heart. Her father, so straight, so proud, so firm. A ruler first, but she'd been born to accept that. Perhaps that's why she'd fallen in love with Reeve. He, too, was a ruler first—of his own life, his own choices.

She didn't know she was weeping as one memory slipped into another. The tears came quietly, in the dark. Closing her eyes, she nearly slept.

"Listen to me." The whisper disturbed her. Brie shook her head. If it was a memory, she didn't want it. But the whisper came again. "It has to be tonight."

"And I tell you it feels wrong."

Not a memory, Brie realized dimly, but still a memory. The voices were there, now, coming through the dark. Through the windows, she realized, that opened up onto the terrace. But she'd heard them before. Her tears dried. She'd heard them before in the dark. This time she recognized them.

Had she been so blind? So stupid? Brie sat up slowly, careful not to make a sound. Yes, she remembered, and she recognized. Her memory was back, but it didn't hurt any longer; it didn't frighten. It enraged.

"We'll follow the plan exactly. Once we have her out,

you take her back to the cottage. We use a stronger drug and keep her tied. There'll be no guard to make a fatal mistake. At one o'clock exactly, a message will be delivered to the prince. There, in the ballroom, he'll know his daughter's been taken again. And he'll know what he has to pay to get her back."

"Deboque."

"And five million francs."

"You and your money." The voice was low and disgusted and too close. Brie gauged the distance to the door and knew she had to wait. "The money means nothing."

"I'll have the satisfaction of knowing Armand had to pay it. After all these years and all this time, I'll have some restitution."

"Revenge." The correction was mild. "And revenge should never be emotional. You'd have been wiser to assassinate him."

"It's been more satisfying to watch him suffer. Just do your part and do it well, or Deboque remains in prison."

"I'll do my part. We'll both have what we want."

They hate each other, Brie realized. Why hadn't she seen it before? It was so clear now, but even tonight, she'd spoken to both of them and suspected nothing.

She sat very still and listened. But there was nothing more than the sound of footsteps receding along the stone. They'd used her and her father. Used her while pretending concern and even affection. She wouldn't be used any longer.

Still, she moved quietly as she crossed the room. She'd find her father and denounce them both. They wouldn't take her again. She twisted the knob and opened the door. And found she wasn't alone.

"Oh, Your Highness." A bit flustered, Janet stepped back and curtsied. "I had no idea you were here. There were some papers—"

"I thought I told you there'd be no more work tonight."

"Yes, Your Highness, but I—"

"Step aside."

It was the tone that gave her away, cold and clear with passion boiling beneath. Janet didn't hesitate. From her simple black bag, she took out a small, efficient gun. Brie didn't even have time to react.

Without fuss, Janet turned and aimed the gun at the guard who stepped from the shadows, his own weapon raised. She fired first, and though there was only a puff of sound, he fell. Even as she started toward the guard, Brie felt the barrel press into her stomach.

"If I shoot you here, you'll die very slowly, very painfully."

"There are other guards," Brie told her as calmly as she could. "They're all through the palace."

"Then unless you want other deaths on your hands, you'll cooperate." Janet knew only one thing—she had to get the princess out of the corridor and away before anyone else happened along. She couldn't risk taking her in the direction of the ballroom. Instead she gave Brie a quick push.

"You'll never get me off the palace grounds unseen," Brie warned her.

"It doesn't matter if they see us. None of the guards would dare shoot when I have a gun to your head." Her plans were in pieces and it wasn't possible to tell her partner. They wouldn't be able to slip a drugged, unconscious Brie out of the dark side entrance watched by the men on their own payroll. They wouldn't be able to close her quietly into the trunk of a waiting car.

The plan had been daring, but it had been organized. Now Janet had nothing.

"What were you planning to do?"

"I was to give you a message privately that the American needed to speak to you, in your room. He would have already been disposed of. Once there, there would have been a hypodermic for you. The rest would have been simple."

"It's not simple now." Brie didn't shudder at the easy way Janet had spoken of killing Reeve. She wouldn't allow herself to shudder. Instead she made herself think as Janet led her closer to the terrace doors. And the dark.

"It's so beautiful!" Eve had decided to give up being sophisticated and enjoy herself. "It must be fantastic to live in a palace every day."

"It's home." Bennett had his arm around her shoulders as they looked down over the high wall. "You know, I've never been to Houston."

"It's nothing like this." Eve took a deep breath before she turned to look at him. He was so handsome, she thought. So sweet. A perfect companion on a late spring night, and yet...

"I'm glad to be here," she said slowly. "But I don't think Prince Alexander likes me."

"Alex?" Bennett gave a shrug. He wasn't going to waste time on Alex when he had a beautiful girl in the moonlight. "He's just a little stuffy, that's all."

She smiled. "You're not. I've read a lot of...interesting things about you."

"All true." He grinned and kissed her hand. "But it's you who interests me now. Eve—" He broke off with a quiet curse as he heard footsteps. "Damn, it's so hard to find a private place around here." Unwilling to be disturbed, he drew Eve into the shadows just as Janet shoved Brie through the doorway.

"I won't go any farther until I know everything." Brie turned, her white dress a slash of light in the shadows. And Bennett saw the gleam of the gun.

"Oh, my God." He covered Eve's mouth with his hand even as she drew the breath to speak. "Listen to me," he whispered, watching his sister. "Go back to the ballroom and get my father or Alex or Reeve MacGee. Get all three if you can. Don't make a sound, just go."

She didn't have to be told twice. She'd seen the gun, as well. Eve nodded so that Bennett would remove his hand. Thinking quickly, she stepped out of her shoes and ran barefoot and silent along the dark side of the building until she came to a set of doors.

"If I have to kill you here," Janet said coolly, "it'll be unpleasant for both of us."

"I want to know why." Brie braced herself against the wall. She didn't know how she'd escape, but she had escaped before.

"Deboque is my lover. I want him back. For you, your father would exchange the devil himself."

Brie narrowed her eyes. Janet Smithers kept her passion well concealed. "How did you get past the security checks? Anyone who's hired to work for my family is—" She stopped herself. The answer was easy. "Loubet, of course."

For the first time, Janet smiled genuinely. "Of course.

Deboque knew of Loubet, of the men Loubet bribed to work for him as well as your father. A little pressure, the threat of exposure, and the eminent minister of state was very cooperative. It helped, too, that he hated your father and looked at the kidnapping as a means of revenge."

"Revenge? Revenge for what?"

"The accident. You remember it now. Your father was driving. He was young, a bit reckless. He and the diplomat suffered only minor injuries, but Loubet..."

"He still limps," Brie murmured.

"Oh, more. Loubet has no children, nor will he ever, even with his young wife. He has yet to tell her, you know. He's afraid she'll leave him. The doctors assure him his problem has nothing to do with the accident. He chooses to believe otherwise."

"So he helped arrange the kidnapping to punish my father? That's mad."

"Hate will make you so. I, on the other hand, hate no one. I simply want my lover back." Janet held the gun so that it caught the moonlight. "I'm quite sane, Your Highness. I'll kill you only if I must."

"And if you do, your lover stays where he is." Brie straightened and called her bluff. "You can't kill me, because I'd be of no use to you dead."

"Quite right." But she aimed the gun again. "Do you

know how painful a bullet can be, though it hits no vital organ?"

"No!" Infuriated, terrified, impulsive, Bennett leaped out of the shadows. He caught both Brie and Janet off guard. Both women froze as he lunged toward the gun. He nearly had it before Janet got off the first shot. The young prince fell without a sound.

"Oh, God, Bennett." Brie was on her knees beside him. "Oh, no, no, Bennett." His blood seeped into the white silk of her dress as she gathered him into her arms. Frantically, she checked for a pulse. "Go ahead and shoot," she hurled at Janet. "You can't do any more to me. I'll see you and your lover in hell for this."

"So you will." Reeve spoke quietly as the doorway was filled with light, men, uniforms and guns.

Janet watched Armand go to his children and the guards stand firm. She held her gun out, butt first. "No dramatics," she said as Reeve stepped forward to take it. "I'm a practical woman."

At a signal from Reeve she was flanked and taken away.

"Oh, Papa." Brie reached out. Armand was on his knees beside Bennett. "He tried to get the gun." Brie pressed her cheek to her brother's hair. "The doctor—"

"He's right here."

"Now, now, Gabriella." Dr. Franco's kind, patient

voice came from behind her. "Let the boy go and give me room."

"I won't leave him. I won't—"

"Don't argue," Bennett said weakly. "I've got the world's worst headache."

She would have wept then, but her father's arm came around her, trembling lightly. "All right, then," she said as she watched Bennett's eyes flutter open. "I'll let him poke and prod at you. God knows I've had my fill of it."

"Brie..." Bennett held her hand a moment. "Any pretty nurses at the hospital?"

"Dozens," she managed.

He sighed and let his eyes close. "Thank God."

Holding out a hand for Alexander, Brie turned into Reeve's arms. She was home at last.

Epilogue

He'd promised her they'd have one last day on the water. That was all, Reeve told himself as the *Liberté* glided in the early-morning wind. They'd have one last day before the fantasy ended. His fantasy.

It had nearly been tragedy, he thought, and couldn't relax even yet. Though Loubet had already been taken when Eve had rushed into the ballroom, Brie had been alone with Deboque's lover.

"I can't believe it's really over," Brie said quietly.

Looking at her, neither could he. But they weren't thinking of the same thing. "It's over."

"Loubet—I could almost feel sorry for him. An illness." Brie thought of his pretty young wife and the shock on her face. "With Janet, an obsession."

"They were users," he reminded her. "Nearly killers. Both Bennett and that guard were lucky."

"I know." Over the past three days, she'd given thanks countless times. "I've killed."

"Brie—"

"No, I've faced it now. Accepted it. I know I was hiding from that, from those horrid days and nights alone in that dark room."

"You weren't hiding," he corrected. "You needed time."

"Now you sound like my doctors." She adjusted the tiller so that they began to tack toward the little cove. "I think parts of my memory, or my feelings were still there. I never told you about the coffee—about Janet's telling me that Nanny always fixed it for me. I never told you, I think, because I never really believed it of her. I couldn't. The bond was too strong."

"But Janet wouldn't understand that."

"She explained to me how Nanny brought it to the office the day I was kidnapped and scolded me a bit. Then she told me I left directly, that she walked me down to my car so that I'd know there had been no chance for anyone else to have doctored it. What she didn't tell me, what I didn't remember until the night of the ball, was that she'd taken the thermos from me and given me a stack of papers to sign. That gave her enough time to do what she had to do."

"But she hadn't counted on the old woman being sharp enough to go to your father with her suspicions after Loubet and Deboque's cousin Henri had picked you up at the little farm."

"Bless Nanny. To think she was watching over me all those weeks when I thought she was just fussing."

"Your father had you well looked after. He wasn't going to risk Loubet's making another move."

"Loubet's plan would have worked if Henri hadn't had a weakness for wine and I hadn't started pouring my soup on the ground. If I'd kept taking the full dose of the drug, I'd never have managed to hold off Henri or break through the boards over the window." She looked down at her hands. The nails were perfect again. They'd suffered badly when she'd fought to pry her way through the window. "Now it's over. I have my life back."

"You're happy with it. That's what matters."

She smiled at him slowly. "Yes, I'm happy with it. You know Christina and Eve are staying a few more days."

"I know your father would like to erect a statue to Eve."

"We've got a lot to be grateful to her for," Brie told him. "I have to say I enjoy watching her bask in the glory."

"The kid was white as a sheet when she got into the ballroom, but she didn't fumble around. She had the story straight and led us right to you."

"I've never thanked you properly." They glided into the little cove and she dropped sail.

"You don't have to thank me."

"But I want to. You gave me a great deal—me and my family. We won't forget it."

"I said you didn't have to thank me." This time his voice was cool as he walked to the rail.

"Reeve…" Brie rose to join him, wishing she were as sure of herself as she intended to sound. "I realize that you're not a citizen of Cordina and therefore not subject to our laws or customs. However, I have a request." She touched her tongue to her top lip. "Since my birthday is only two weeks away, we can call it a royal request if you like. It's customary for members of the royal family to have a request granted on the anniversary of their birth."

"A request." He pulled out a cigarette and lit it. "Which is?"

She liked him like this, a bit annoyed, a bit aloof. It would make it easier. "Our engagement is very popular, wouldn't you agree?"

He gave a short laugh. "Yeah."

"For myself, I have to confess I'm quite fond of the diamond you gave me."

"Keep it," he said carelessly. "Consider it a gift."

She looked down at it, then at the ring on her right hand. No more conflicting loyalties, she mused. Her emotions were very clear. "I intend to." She smiled as he shot her a cool look. "You know, I have a number of connections. There could be quite a bit of trouble with your passport, your visa, even your flight back to America."

Pitching the cigarette into the sea, he turned completely around. "What are you getting at?"

"I think it would be much simpler all around if you married me. In fact, I'm planning to insist."

He leaned back against the rail and watched her. He couldn't read her now—perhaps his own feelings prevented it. She was speaking as Princess Gabriella, cool, calm and confident. "Is that so?"

"Yes. If you cooperate, I'm sure we can work things out to mutual advantage."

"I'm not interested in advantages."

"Nonsense." She brushed this off, but her palms were damp. "It would be possible for us to spend six months in Cordina and six months in America," she went on. "I believe there must be a certain amount of compromise in any marriage. You agree?"

Negotiations. He'd carried out plenty of them as a cop. "Maybe."

She swallowed quietly, then went on speaking in an

easy, practical tone. "Naturally, I have a lot of obligations, but when Alexander marries, his wife will assume some of them. In the meantime, it's hardly more than having a job, really."

Enough, he thought, of details and plans. Enough negotiating. He wanted it plain. "Simplify it." He took a step forward and she took one back.

"I don't know what you mean."

"Tell me what you want and why."

"You," she said keeping her chin up. "Because I love you and I have ever since I was sixteen and you kissed me on the terrace with the roses and moonlight."

He wanted to touch her cheek, but he didn't, not yet. Not just yet. "You're not sixteen anymore, and this isn't a fairy tale."

"No."

Was she smiling? he wondered. Didn't she know how badly he needed her to mean it? "There won't be a palace waiting for you in America."

"There's a house with a big front porch." She took another step back. "Don't make me beg. If you don't want me, say so."

This time she spoke as a woman, not so confident, not so cool. He had what he needed.

"When you were sixteen and I waltzed with you, it was like a dream." He took her hands. "I never forgot it. When I came back and kissed you again, it was real. I've never wanted anything more."

Her hands were firm on his. "And I've never wanted anyone more."

"Marry me, Brie, and sit on the porch with me. If we can have that, I can live with Her Serene Highness Gabriella."

She took both of his hands to her face and kissed them, one at a time. "It isn't a fairy tale, but sometimes life is happy ever after."

* * * * *

Fall under the spell of *New York Times*
bestselling author

Nora Roberts

and her MacGregor novels

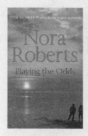 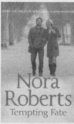 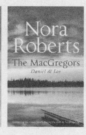 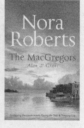

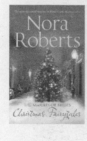 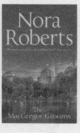 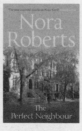 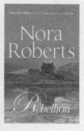

400 million of her books in print worldwide

www.millsandboon.co.uk

BL/267/CRF

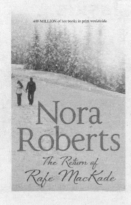
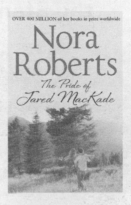
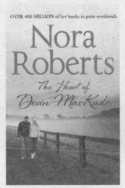
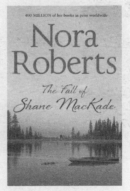

Introducing
the Stanislaskis...

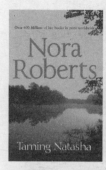
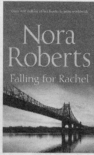
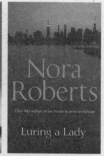

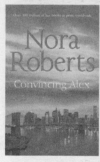
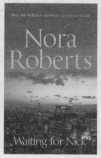
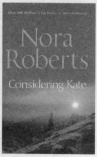

**Fall under the spell of *New York Times*
bestselling author**

Nora Roberts

www.millsandboon.co.uk

MILLS & BOON®

Fancy some more Mills & Boon books?

Well, good news!

We're giving you

15% OFF

your next eBook or paperback book purchase
on the Mills & Boon website.

So hurry, visit the website today and type **GIFT15**
in at the checkout for your exclusive 15% discount.

www.millsandboon.co.uk/gift15

MILLS & BOON®

Why shop at millsandboon.co.uk?

Each year, thousands of romance readers find their perfect read at millsandboon.co.uk. That's because we're passionate about bringing you the very best romantic fiction. Here are some of the advantages of shopping at www.millsandboon.co.uk:

* **Get new books first**—you'll be able to buy your favourite books one month before they hit the shops

* **Get exclusive discounts**—you'll also be able to buy our specially created monthly collections, with up to 50% off the RRP

* **Find your favourite authors**—latest news, interviews and new releases for all your favourite authors and series on our website, plus ideas for what to try next

* **Join in**—once you've bought your favourite books, don't forget to register with us to rate, review and join in the discussions

Visit **www.millsandboon.co.uk**
for all this and more today!